ABOUT

"Sally Jenkins knows now to build a story. She takes the mundane, and makes it intriguing. She hooks the reader, and reels him in ... her capacity for twisting each tale's ending is nothing short of phenomenal." - Readers' Favorite Book Review Website.

Sally's stories have been successful in a range of competitions and many have been published in magazines. Her tales play with the quirks and twists in our everyday lives.

Bedsit Three, Sally's debut novel won the Ian Govan Award and is a slice of British psychological noir, about relationships and the instinct of parents to want the best for their children.

Her second novel, **The Promise**, tells the story of a vow made in prison thirty years ago and the shockwaves it causes three decades later.

Sally lives in north Birmingham with her husband. The wilderness of Sutton Park is close by, a wonderful place for wandering, plotting and creating characters. By day Sally works in IT but after hours she lets her imagination and pen run riot. And when she's not hammering at the keyboard, she gets her exercise bell ringing and walking.

Find Sally on Twitter @sallyjenkinsuk
or follow her blog at http://www.sally-jenkins.com

Hit or Miss?
33 Coffee Break Stories

SALLY JENKINS

Hit or Miss?

Copyright © 2022 Sally Jenkins

ISBN 13: 9798352491959

ALL RIGHTS RESERVED

All content herein remains the copyright of Sally Jenkins, 2022.

The right of the author to be identified as the author of this work has been asserted by her in accordance with the relevant copyright legislation in her country of residence and generally under section 6bis of the Berne Convention for the Protection of Literary and Artistic Works.

This book may not, by way of trade or otherwise, be lent, re-sold, hired out, reproduced or otherwise circulated without prior consent of the author.

This work is a work of fiction. Name, places and incidents are either products of the author's imaginations or are used fictitiously. Any resemblance to any event, incident, location or person (living or dead) is entirely coincidental.

For further information and details about volume sales, please see the author's website at www.sally-jenkins.com.

"I'll give you the whole secret to short story writing. Here it is. Rule 1: Write stories that please yourself. There is no Rule 2."

O. Henry 1862 – 1910
American Short Story Writer

Contents

INTRODUCTION 1

ONE LAST JOB 3

MIDNIGHT MOMENTS 8

TWO COUPLES AND A CAKE 12

GUINEA PIG AND CHIPS 18

STEP COUNTER 25

MATCHSTICKS AND GLUE 31

THE TRIP COLLECTOR 40

COFFEE CAPERS 48

TRAVELLING WITH TIM 53

NIGHT LIFE 58

CASUALTY 65

CLOTHES TO DIE FOR 71

MAN VERSUS MACHINE 79

THE PERSONAL SHOPPER 84

THE CHECKLIST 90

THE SAME BUT DIFFERENT 96

LOOKALIKE	104
FEAR OF FLYING	109
CAREER CHANGE	113
LOCAL FLASH FICTION	119
MARATHON MADNESS	125
ALL THE LIFT I NEEDED	129
EMERALD WRITING WORKSHOPS FLASH FICTION	133
FRONTLINE RESPONSE	143
RENOUNCING THE EMPIRE	148
OLD COMEDIANS NEVER DIE	154
NOBODY'S HERO	160
ADAPTING NOT CHEATING	164

INTRODUCTION

Every short story writer has a drawer full of tales looking for a home. These are the stories that didn't quite make the competition shortlist or that weren't sufficiently pleasing to magazine editors. We continue to work on these stories and resubmit them elsewhere. It might take several iterations of this rewrite/resubmit procedure before a particular story finds a home. Sometimes that home never materialises and the story gets labelled a 'Miss'. This doesn't mean the story is bad or without merit; it simply means it didn't land on the right desk at the right time.

In this book I have brought together both my short story 'Hits' and some of my short story 'Misses'. I invite you to read each story and make up your own mind about its merit before discovering whether it was a 'Hit' or a 'Miss' and which publications or competitions deemed it to be so.

Judging the merits of a story is subjective. Rarely do we unanimously adore or hate the same thing. I'd love to know whether you agree with the 'Hit' or 'Miss' verdicts in this book and if there is a particular story that you enjoyed. If you are happy to share your thoughts on the Amazon review page of *Hit or Miss?* (without spoilers!) that would be fantastic.

Sally Jenkins.

ONE LAST JOB

Sly stood in front of the hall mirror and admired his work uniform. The blue of the fabric was so dark that it was almost black and provided the perfect background to the shiny brass buttons. He adjusted the peaked cap so that it shaded his eyes.

His new boss, Martin, had stressed the importance of appearance. "We don't want to advertise to our clients or the cashiers that you're fresh out of Strangeways. So, no tattoos on display, no smoking and only speak if you're spoken to. If you need to contact me, use the radio discreetly and don't start a panic. Your job is to observe what's going on in the public part of the bank and let me know immediately anything unexpected happens."

Sly pinned a name badge on the breast pocket of his jacket. It displayed the subtle diamond logo of Souter's Private Bank and was printed with the name 'Sylvester Chambers', making him look the genuine article, a bank security guard. His collar was buttoned right up and he had a tightly knotted diamond print tie. He checked his watch; it was time to leave the house and drive to the bank.

Sly crammed his bulky frame into his wife's old Fiesta. As usual Kathleen had moaned at him before handing over her keys. "You promised me a top of the range convertible when you did that last bank job and what happened? You got put inside and I had to buy the Fiesta off a dodgy dealer with my cleaning wages."

The rush hour traffic had become worse over the seven years he'd spent in prison and Sly had seriously underestimated the amount of time it would take to drive to Souter's. Workmen in hi-vis jackets were installing temporary traffic lights on the main road into the town centre and Sly had to wait whilst they faffed around with cables, cones and road signs. He imagined Martin looking at his watch, getting edgy and wondering why he'd put his trust in an old ex-con like Sly.

Despite him being ten minutes late, no one had stolen the prime parking space right outside the bank. The manager and most of the staff parked in the bank's private car park at the back of the building because it was secure. But Martin had said that Sly should park at the front.

"I thought you'd let me down," Martin hissed when Sly entered the banking hall. "We can't operate without a security guard on duty."

Sly started to apologise but Martin interrupted him. "Not now, not in front of the customers. Remember, stay in touch via the radio. Tell me anything and everything that could stop things running smoothly out here. I'll be watching you on CCTV to start with."

Sly leaned against the wall and watched the customers come and go. They were all well-heeled. In the old days he might have tried to pick a purse or two from the open shopping bags carried by the older ladies. But today it wasn't worth the risk. Souter's would be his last job and then retirement beckoned. Soon open-necked shirts, shorts and sandals would be the order of the day; he and Kathleen were planning to immigrate to the Costa del Sol.

"Stand up straight! Look authentic instead of like an ex-con." Martin's voice crackled through the radio, making Sly jump.

He pulled his shoulders back and took a walk around the banking hall. Martin obviously didn't think he was up to the job but Sly was going to prove him wrong.

It was ten to ten according to the clock on the wall. The initial surge of early customers had died down and the three cashiers were talking amongst themselves. Sly began to get bored of waiting and watching. His mind wandered back to Spain. Two of the gang members from his last bank job had escaped there, it was only Sly who had got banged up and, like a professional, he hadn't squealed on the others. They still had his share of the proceeds and he'd get it just as soon as his early release probation period was up and he could go abroad.

The radio sprang into life again and Martin's voice relayed the message Sly had been expecting. "The CCTV has gone down. You're the only eyes I have in the hall. Don't let me down."

Sly looked at the clock again, one minute to ten.

HIT OR MISS?

Not long to go. The cashiers were laughing at something that had been on television the previous evening.

A man came in with a bowler hat and briefcase. He nodded at Sly and Sly returned the acknowledgement, keeping his face neutral. The man put his briefcase on the counter next to the middle cashier, clicked the fasteners open and reached inside.

Sly's probation officer had got him this job. Martin was her son as well as head of security at Souter's and she'd persuaded him that Sly had the right experience. Martin had been concerned that at sixty-two Sly was too old and his reactions would be slow. The younger man's negative attitude had irritated Sly so he'd hatched a plan to get himself to Spain a little bit sooner and hopefully with more cash.

At ten o'clock the scream and alarm bells started simultaneously.

"Hand the cash over quickly!" bawled the man in the bowler hat, pointing a gun at the terrified cashier.

She was thrusting bundles of notes into a carrier bag and the other two cashiers were passing the contents of their tills to her. For a second, Sly was frozen to the spot and then the adrenalin kicked in. He recognised the gun as a fake, just as Martin had promised it would be.

"I might be organising a robbery on my own bank but I won't put the lives of any of my staff at risk," his boss had said at their planning meeting. "Your job is to keep any customers well back and then make it look as though the raider is forcing you to drive him away at gun point."

As planned the bowler hatted man put the gun menacingly to Sly's head and, for the benefit of the cashiers, appeared to frog march him out of the bank. As the pair entered the rotating door, the massed blue ranks of the police became visible outside. Sly pushed forward on the glass eagerly but bowler hat man tried to force the door to go backwards. Two constables shoved the door from outside and propelled Sly and the raider into the arms of their colleagues.

"Thanks for the tip-off, Sly," said the Detective Inspector later, as he served the ex-con tea in his office. "You've helped us catch a nice little trio, a bent probation officer, a dodgy head of bank security and a career criminal."

Souter's Bank wanted to publicly honour Sly and give him a security consultancy role. Sly declined; no ex-con wants to become famous as a grass and the world of real work didn't appeal. But he did accept the £20,000 reward, paid it into a Euro bank account and booked two plane tickets to Spain.

Hit or Miss?

Hit!

One Last Job was rejected by *Take a Break Fiction Feast* in July 2015 but published in *The Weekly News* in October 2015.

MIDNIGHT MOMENTS

A blanket of heat engulfed Gillian as she stepped from the plane onto the airport tarmac. The enveloping warmth was a sharp contrast to the dismal grey day she'd left behind.

Her daughter thought she was mad. "You're having a mid-life Shirley Valentine crisis," she'd said when her mother announced her decision to quit her job and run away to the Greek island.

"No, I'm not. I just can't stand work and that stupid marketing director any longer. I've spent two years branding Midnight Moments as *the* chocolates to buy for special occasions. And now he wants to reduce their price! He thinks it will increase sales and make more profit. I think it will ruin the image of the brand."

"So, get a new job instead of running away."

"I have – my new job is waiting for me in Corfu. You are grown up. I don't have a husband to consider any more. I'm going to change my life. Besides, Sue needs me."

Sue, Gillian's oldest friend, had married a Greek after being swept off her feet on a back-packing trip thirty years previously. Now widowed, she needed help running her small gift shop in Corfu town.

The taxi taking Gillian from the airport darted through the narrow streets. History oozed from every pore of the old stone walls and that wonderful sunshine was slowing life towards a lazy post-lunch siesta – shops were shutting and the only people on the streets studied maps and carried cameras. Mad dogs and Englishmen, thought Gillian.

"It's great to have you here!" Sue squealed, as the taxi driver unloaded Gillian's luggage.

"Show me your emporium!" Gillian commanded when Sue's bear hug finally weakened.

Sue had just closed for the afternoon but she proudly showed Gillian the business that she and her late husband, Claas, had built up.

"I had to employ a young girl last summer after Claas died," Sue's voice faltered. "The evenings are too busy for one person to manage during the peak. But it will be much more fun to have you here this season instead!"

Gillian glowed. It was great to be wanted. Her old boss had never shown any appreciation. Sue may be paying peanuts but Gillian knew that the emotional rewards for working here would be worth so much more than her old salary.

"Our customers are mostly tourists," Sue went on, "children with holiday spending money and adults wanting souvenirs and presents to take home."

Gillian glanced around the shelves of the dimly-lit

shop. They were loaded with fridge magnets, racks of postcards, cuddly animals and tea towels – most of them emblazoned with images of Corfu.

Gillian could almost smell the freedom around her, the freedom to be involved in something that didn't need umpteen meetings and emails to decide one small thing.

"I've also ordered some English confectionary," Sue said. "Lots of the kids come in wanting their favourite chocolate bar and I have to turn them away. But this summer I'll be selling them – it should encourage customers to keep coming back to the shop."

Gillian nodded.

At 5pm Sue unlocked the shop door again and customers started to mooch in. Gillian made a point of engaging them in conversation, about themselves and where they came from – and, after such personal treatment, they usually bought something. Sue was pleased and said takings for the evening were higher than usual.

The next morning, over breakfast on the sun-warmed balcony, the two women reminisced until the sound of aggressive, repeated beeping from the other end of the narrow street grew too loud to ignore.

Parked cars had forced an approaching delivery lorry to abandon its effort to reverse right up to the gift shop and the driver was now cursing as he manhandled several large cardboard boxes up the road to the shop.

"It's the confectionary!" Sue ran downstairs to meet the delivery man.

After signing his sheet of paper, she turned to Gillian.

"We open soon, could you get this priced and on display quickly? You're the marketing guru so I'll let you choose the best way of doing it. There is a chiller cabinet if you think the chocolate needs keeping cool."

Gillian relished the opportunity to use her initiative. She grabbed a sharp knife, cut through the brown tape sealing the first box and then groaned loudly as the cardboard flaps opened. The purple and black boxes stared up at her mockingly.

"I want to put a lower price on these," Sue said, looking over Gillian's shoulder at the cellophane sheathed Midnight Moments boxes. "They're a luxury product but selling them cheaper will give me higher sales."

Kneeling on the floor, Gillian raised her head and howled in anguish.

Hit or Miss?

Miss.

Various versions of Midnight Moments were rejected between 2012 and 2015 by *Woman's Weekly*, *Take a Break Fiction Feast*, *The Weekly News*, *My Weekly* and *Prima*. It remains one of my favourite stories.

TWO COUPLES AND A CAKE

Edna felt a wave of anxiety when she saw her granddaughter's wedding cake. It stood tall and elegant on the top table at the wedding breakfast - three tiers of white royal icing festooned with a rope of pink sugar roses. It was perfect.

The room was filling up with guests and there was a lively buzz of conversation and laughter.

Edna clutched George's arm. "There are too many people," she whispered. "I'm going to tell Naomi her offer was very generous but I'd rather stay out of the limelight."

"No," George said gently. "Once we're up there you'll enjoy it."

Edna sighed and took her seat at the table. It was that old wedding photo that had prompted Naomi to share her big day. Edna had kept it hidden at the back of the sideboard for seventy years. It showed a bride and groom with a beautiful three-tier cake and had never been framed. Her mother hadn't understood why.

"It's a lovely photo, Edna," she'd said when the prints came back from the photographer. "You look radiant and George is handsome in his uniform. It's the best photo of the lot."

"It wasn't real though, was it?" Edna had argued.

"It was as real as anything can be with a war on. Your Dad spent hours getting it perfect and several people have asked if they can borrow it."

"Then it was lucky he could put it back together. George was mortified at what happened."

Edna's father had unveiled his masterpiece in the shed on the morning of the wedding. It was beautiful but there'd been no chance to warn George about it before the ceremony.

"Soup, madam." The waiter made Edna jump by placing a bowl of steaming liquid in front of her.

Edna glanced across the room. Naomi was pointing at the cake and giving her grandmother a thumbs-up sign. Edna awkwardly returned the gesture and wondered if Naomi would be disappointed if she suggested backing out now.

After all these years George had re-discovered the photo in the sideboard when their granddaughter and her fiancé were visiting. He'd told the young couple the whole story.

Edna and George's wedding had been very different to this grand affair. Everyone had chipped in with their rations to ensure that there was a cake. Edna's mother had fretted about whether she had the ingredients to bake one large enough to feed all the guests and the cake-making day had been fraught with tension. There could be no second chances with the

HIT OR MISS?

frugal recipe - if it failed to rise, burned or got spoiled it would still have to be served to thirty guests. There had been no disaster but still Edna's mother worried.

"That's as big as I could make it." Her mother had pointed to the golden sponge on the cooling rack. "But a photograph of you and George cutting into something no bigger than a fairy cake will look ridiculous."

Then Edna's dad had come up trumps - or so he thought. He'd spent a long night in the garden hut, refusing to let Edna see what he was doing.

The reception was in the church hall and there were sandwiches and salad from the coupons that neighbours had been saving. There were even some tinned pears. If only she'd managed to tell George about the cake everything might have been perfect.

After the meal Edna's father carried in the cake and placed it in front of the bride and groom. A chorus of cheering and clapping erupted when the guests saw it.

"Perfect." George whispered in her ear. "Fruitcake, marzipan and royal icing - what more could a man want on his wedding day?"

Edna was about to explain when he'd placed his lips on hers and kissed her sweetly. Then there was no time to speak because they were being beckoned forward to face the photographer. They held the knife together and smiled, the flash bulb popped and the guests cheered again. The resulting picture showed the two of them in their wedding finery holding a large shiny knife; the tip of the blade was resting on the bottom layer of a three-tier cake. Painted pink flowers cascaded down the tiers and delicate white columns supported the top two cakes.

As the flash died away Edna felt George increase his pressure on the knife and realised he was trying to cut the cake.

"This icing's rock solid," he muttered.

"No, George. It's not …"

George pushed on the knife with all his weight and the cake shot away from him, landing on the floor.

There was silence in the hall.

Edna gazed, horrified, at the mess of cardboard and plaster. In the middle of it all was the small broken sponge cake - it had been hidden beneath the bottom tier.

"Dad made a cardboard cake," she sobbed, "to cover Mum's small sponge, for the sake of the photos."

George apologised and apologised to anyone who'd listen. Edna's mum rescued most of the sponge and no one objected to being served broken cake.

Edna had blamed herself for the fiasco and had hidden the picture to block out the memory.

Now, the butterflies in Edna's stomach were making it difficult to enjoy the roast beef and Yorkshire pudding. She glanced at George. His plate was nearly empty and he looked completely relaxed. Didn't he realise that in a few minutes they'd have to stand up in front of all these people they didn't know? Many of them were Naomi's and Mick's friends from university and George and Edna had never met Mick's family.

Naomi had invited her grandparents to do something that was not part of a traditional wedding and everyone would wonder what on earth was going on.

The waiters poured sparkling wine and Naomi's dad stood up to give his speech. Edna heard none of it. The father of the bride finished and was replaced by Mick and then the best man. A lot of applause and loud laughter followed.

"The cutting of the cake!" announced the best man.

Naomi and Mick stood up.

Naomi cleared her throat. "My grandparents had a very different wedding to this one."

She talked about rationing and the cardboard cake. At Edna's request she didn't mention how things had gone terribly wrong. Instead, she stressed how wartime brides had missed out on the wedding day pleasures now taken for granted.

"So, Nan and Grandpa didn't cut a proper cake on their big day. Today, I'd like to put that right and invite them up here to help us cut ours."

The applause was deafening. As Edna stood anxiously beside the cake, she felt a great wave of warmth from the guests and her nerves disappeared. Smiling and holding the knife together, she and George made the first cut and then Naomi and Mick sliced into the cake too. Flash bulbs went off all around the room.

"Now we can display *two* photographs of us with a wedding cake," George whispered as they sat back down.

Edna nodded - the joyful lump in her throat meant she couldn't speak.

<u>Hit or Miss?</u>

Hit!

A version of 'Two Couples and a Cake' was published in *The People's Friend* in March 2015 under the title, 'The Icing on the Cake'.

The story was inspired by a war-time rationing wedding cake anecdote, told to me by my mum.

GUINEA PIG AND CHIPS

The usual cacophony of squeaking greeted Karl as he entered the barn.

"Nice to see you! To see you, nice!" he called and gave a twirl.

The guinea pigs' stoneware food dishes were empty, bar a few stray droppings which Karl emptied into a black sack. Then he re-filled the bowls with the mix of lettuce, cucumber, parsnip and cauliflower the farmer had given him.

Whilst the furry heads were busy investigating their evening meal, Karl pulled a plastic carrier bag from the pocket of his overcoat – it contained the spoils of his afternoon searching for dandelion leaves in the park. Two small children had helped him until their mother noticed, took them by the hand and marched them away.

"Strange men in dirty overcoats are dangerous," she'd said in a loud, angry voice and Karl had felt sad.

But the guinea pigs sent that sadness away. He tempted a small brown and white one away from the food dish by trailing a fresh green dandelion leaf under her nose. These poor animals were captives and Karl wanted to make their lives as bearable as possible. But nothing made up for not being able to run free.

The farmer had been reluctant to employ him. There'd been a meeting with Karl's probation officer and social worker and they'd talked about him as if he hadn't been there.

"I won't have an ex-con working here, especially one that's educationally subnormal like he is," the farmer had said gruffly. "It's a children's farm - if word gets out no one will come."

"What about after the public leaves? There must be a lot of clearing up after the visitors and cleaning out of the animals," the probation officer speculated. "Isn't it hard to get people to do that sort of work?"

Karl sat quietly, scared to open his mouth in case he said the wrong thing. He loved animals and was desperate to work with them.

"Aye, you're right. It's dirty graft and no-one wants to do it." The farmer paused. "Did you say there's a scheme to subsidise his wages – being as he's fresh out of jail?"

A lot of official talk followed, which Karl didn't understand, forms were filled in, hands were shaken and Karl had a job for three hours every evening after the farm had closed.

Each day he got the awful parts of his work done first. He looked forward to the guinea pigs whilst he cleaned toilets, emptied litter bins and mopped the floor of the cafeteria.

Karl picked up one of the animals and stroked its sleek white coat as it nibbled the green leaf in his hand. It had red eyes. He used to think that meant it was blind but, by using the internet at the hostel computer club, he'd discovered that it probably wasn't. The red eyes actually meant it was albino.

"Put it back and get finished. I want to lock up." The farmer didn't understand that his animals needed a little bit of love now and again.

Obediently, Karl slipped the guinea pig back into the enclosure where it scurried into the miniature school building. Then he gave the barn a sweep and the farmer padlocked the doors. There was a brightly painted sign above them, "Guinea Pig Village". Like the things he saw on the internet, Karl could read it without any difficulty. Reading was the best thing he'd learned during his five years inside.

"In Peru, they eat guinea pigs," said the farmer. "It was on TV last night. They leave the claws and head on, so it's staring up at you from the plate. You gnaw the meat off the bones, like eating a chicken leg. I might try serving it in the café here."

"You're making it up!" Karl put his hands over his ears.

"Check for yourself. It's true."

Karl eyed the farmer distrustfully and thought about the energetic small animals, with their intelligent eyes, ending up on a dinner table. Back at the hostel, in the computer club room, he typed into a search engine. A series of images appeared of small, golden-brown deep-fried bodies lying on their backs with legs splayed out. One was on a plate with a great pile of chips and another was resting on a bed of mashed potatoes. Karl's body shook. He wanted to punch these over-happy, smiley diners raising their glasses to the camera. The grotesque chef who'd skewered a whole row of the animals over a barbeque deserved to die. He wondered if the farmer meant it about serving guinea pig in the café.

The next day Karl wielded his toilet brush with venom and rushed through his mopping and disinfecting to get to the Guinea Pig Village earlier. He needed extra time with his friends. As usual they swarmed over to the fresh food he brought. His heart swelled with happiness.

"Hey, Snowy! You're missing your dinner."

The white animal he'd stroked the day before was half-hidden by the model sweetshop in the guinea pig village. Karl gently touched the pale fur on its bottom, which stuck out from behind the building. It didn't move. Karl's hand trembled as he gently lifted the motionless animal. He laid it on his hand and trailed his fingers over the white hair. The animal didn't react. A huge lump sat in Karl's throat and then disintegrated into sobs that were impossible to control.

Snowy had known nothing but the inside of this barn with its miniature greengrocer's, a church without stained glass and empty shells of houses. He'd never run outside in the wild or burrowed in the desert. It wasn't fair.

Karl's probation officer had brought him to the farm during the day once, before he started work here. Karl had seen the children prodding and poking the guinea pigs. The animals got no peace until the lights were turned out in the evening. It reminded Karl of prison. Everything there was artificially manufactured, from the work they did, to the library and education classes. It was pretending to be the same as in the outside world but none of it was. And all the time psychiatrists, prison wardens and other unknown people watched, asked questions and wrote things on clipboards – like the kids snatching at the guinea pigs.

Now Snowy was with the angels, in a better place. Karl put the dead animal gently in his backpack. If he left it here, the farmer would just toss the body in the bin or, even worse, eat it.

Karl studied the remaining guinea pigs. The initial food excitement had abated and they'd returned to sniffing around the enclosure. He didn't want the rest of them to die without ever tasting freedom. Imagine if he had died in prison?

Back at the hostel, Karl took out his best shirt, the one he'd worn at that first meeting with the farmer, and wrapped Snowy's body in it. There was a small garden behind the hostel but it was late and Karl discovered the tool shed was locked. He took a large spoon from the kitchen and started digging where the earth was soft in a flower bed beneath a deep red rose bush. He dug until he reached the roots but the hole still wasn't big enough to hold the shirt-wrapped guinea pig. The whole shirt was too bulky to bury. Karl tore off a single sleeve to act as Snowy's shroud and slipped the package into the newly dug grave. He covered the body in earth and patted it down on top. Then he used two twigs and an elastic band to fashion a cross and placed it on the grave.

The following day he went to Guinea Pig Village before doing his horrible cleaning jobs.

"Nice to see you! To see you, nice!" Karl's usual greeting caught in his throat.

The guinea pigs squeaked back at him and he filled their food bowls. Then he started examining the walls of the barn.

"There's a lovely field out there," he said, "with lots of places for you to burrow and do exactly as you please. There's plenty of grass to eat and I might stop by with the odd vegetable treat. There'll be no-one prodding and poking you."

His fingers found a slightly rotten panel. He pulled out his penknife and started to create a small hole in the soft wood at floor level.

"The internet says you should live wild in Peru. I can't send you there but this field is the next best thing. And we don't eat guinea pigs in England – you'll be perfectly safe."

Karl stood up and faced his charges. "Who wants to be first? Don't all squeak at once."

He picked up one of the fatter animals and placed it by the hole. "Through there to freedom."

The guinea pig stood in front of the hole, its nose twitching and its ears alert. Then it scurried into a dark corner of the barn. Karl tracked the animal down and cradled it gently.

"I was scared too when they first let me out," he whispered. "For years everything had been taken care of for me. I just did what I was told. Then suddenly the door opened and I had choices. Now I feel properly alive and that's how it'll be for you."

Karl pushed the animal through the hole. Then he lay flat on his stomach and peered after it. The guinea pig was about ten feet away, nibbling grass. Karl smiled.

One by one he lifted the others from their enclosure and pushed them through the gap in the wood. He looked out when the last one was gone. The field was dotted with brown, white and black guinea pigs enjoying their first taste of freedom.

"Have you finished?" the farmer was calling from the door.

"Yes." Karl stood up, brushed himself down and went outside.

Hit or Miss?

Miss.

Over the course of three years (2012 – 2015) this story failed to make the grade in competitions organised by *The Writers' and Artists' Yearbook*, *Writers' News*, *The Tom-Gallon Trust Award* and *Words Mag*.
When I wrote this story, I had in my mind's eye a guinea pig 'village' on a children's farm which I'd visited several years earlier with my young daughters and also the guinea pigs I had as pets when I was a child.

STEP COUNTER

Exercise wasn't Eric's first love. He knew he should do more. His expanding girth wasn't healthy but at fifty-nine he considered himself too old to start running around in Lycra. Sitting now, in the park café with his newspaper and bacon roll, he watched the world race past him in a blur of trainers, walking boots and bicycles. He couldn't understand this obsession with movement. His wife, Christine, had become addicted to Zumba and now she spent her whole life rushing. Rushing to get home from work, to get changed and off to her exercise class. Rushing round the supermarket early on a Saturday so she didn't miss the aerobic dance session with her favourite teacher. Eric justified his slow existence by remembering the first line of that old poem, "What is this life if, full of care, we have no time to stand and stare."

"Eric!" Christine had walked into the café and was

squeezing between the tables to reach him. She looked like a woman on a mission.

Eric sighed and put his paper down.

"I've got a present for you. These were on special offer in the sports shop." Christine sat on the empty chair next to him and put a small carrier bag on the table.

A feeling of foreboding descended. He had no need of anything from the sports shop. This must be yet another attempt by his wife to get him exercising. Inside the bag was a box. Inside the box was a small, black plastic thing with a tiny screen and a belt hook.

"It's a step counter!" Christine said excitedly. "It records how many steps you do each day. The target is ten thousand and it links to your phone and sends encouraging messages."

"Did you keep the receipt?" Eric asked. He had no intention of using this step counter thing.

"No." Christine's voice was firm. "If you won't take more exercise for yourself then do it for me. I don't want you to die of a heart attack."

That evening Christine insisted Eric accompany her as she walked the dog.

"We haven't got a dog!" All this exercise had addled his wife's brain.

"Old Mrs Holdsworth can't get out much now. I told her you would walk her dog morning and evening to increase your step count. We'll go together tonight as it's the first time." Christine handed Eric his jacket and made sure he had the step counter clipped to his trouser waistband.

They walked to the park and then Christine insisted they walk twice around its perimeter before going back home. Dotty, Mrs Holdsworth's

Dalmatian, was obedient and well-behaved. They let her off the lead and she zig-zagged around in front of them.

"She's doing twice as many steps as us," Eric said.

"Once you're a bit fitter you'll want to go faster and further too. Come on don't dawdle." Christine increased her walking speed.

Eric began to pant as he tried to keep up with his wife and Dotty. By the time he got home he was exhausted. He sank into his chair to check the football results on his phone. The little envelope symbol was highlighted at the top of the screen; he had a message.

He swiped the screen and read the text. "4,302 steps completed. Only 5,698 to go to reach today's target. Go for it!"

"Go for it yourself," Eric muttered and swiped the message away.

The next morning Christine sent him out before breakfast to walk Dotty. By the time he got back she'd already gone to work but had left him a note in shouty capital letters: "WALK DOTTY WHILST I'M AT ZUMBA THIS EVENING. I WILL CHECK YOUR STEP COUNT LATER. AND DON'T TAKE THE LIFT AT WORK – USE THE STAIRS."

Eric groaned.

When he went to collect Dotty for her evening walk there was a long pause after he knocked on Mrs Holdsworth's door. For a couple of minutes Eric thought he was off the hook. Mrs Holdsworth must have gone out and therefore Dotty couldn't have her walk. Then his heart sank as he heard footsteps in the hall and a little bark of excitement.

"Sorry I took so long," Mrs Holdsworth said. "I was putting Dotty's lead on so that she'd be all ready for you."

Eric took the proffered lead and waved goodbye to Mrs Holdsworth. At the park he let Dotty run free and they repeated their two-perimeter circuit. Eric looked longingly at the café where a few people were lounging, enjoying the last of the day's sunshine. He wondered how exercise fanatics kept up with news and sport – these two walks a day meant Eric had no time to read his paper and certainly no time to stand and stare.

At the end of the week Christine logged into his Step Counter account on the internet and reviewed his progress.

"You're not quite there," she frowned. "Your best day was Thursday with 9,500 steps."

"That was the day I had to go round to the cake shop and help Jim fetch cakes for his birthday," Eric explained.

Christine looked at her husband's belly and her frown deepened. "Tomorrow's Saturday. I'm sure Dotty won't mind three walks."

Christine accompanied Eric on the first two walks but said she'd do the cooking whilst he did the third walk alone. "After all," she said, "I have done a Zumba class today as well."

"Dotty *is* getting spoiled!" Mrs Holdsworth said when Eric turned up on her doorstep again. She handed over the lead and, this time, a ball as well. "My grandson left it behind. He and Dotty were playing with it in the garden. She might like to chase it in the park."

Eric slipped the ball into his pocket. He didn't

fancy all the bending and stretching involved in playing ball with a dog, just as he didn't fancy walking all the way around the park twice more. There was a large grassy area just inside the park and a couple of dogs were racing across it after sticks. Dotty paused and looked longingly. Eric watched for a few seconds. He took the step counter off his waistband, looked at the count, thought about how slowly the numbers mounted and then looked at the dogs racing across the grass like Olympic sprinters. He smiled to himself, fiddled around with Dotty's collar, removed her lead and then threw the ball as far as he could. Dotty sped off and returned thirty seconds later and dropped the ball at his feet. Eric picked up the ball and threw it again. The man next to him struck up a conversation and, between them each throwing balls for their dogs, they discussed the performance of all the local football teams and also had time to simply stand and stare.

When the man left, Eric put the lead back on a reluctant Dotty and removed the step counter from her collar. He looked at the screen: 17,102 steps.

"Yes!" Eric shouted and punched the air. Christine could not argue with this solid proof that he'd increased his physical activity.

"You are a star, Dotty," he said and they walked home.

Hit or Miss?

Hit!

This story was published in *The Weekly News* in 2018. It was inspired by the growing numbers of us carrying various bits of technology to encourage us to walk ten thousand steps a day. Incidentally, did you know that there is no medical evidence to say that ten thousand steps provide the optimum amount of exercise? It is an arbitrary number of steps devised by the Japanese makers of the first pedometer in the 1960s.

MATCHSTICKS AND GLUE

The once bottle green front door had faded to the blotched appearance of army camouflage. Paint of the same dirty hue peeled from the window frames. But Red Cardinal polish shone brightly from the doorstep like a welcome beacon - could Doreen have guessed he was coming home today? He'd written only a week ago to say now the war was over they expected to be demobbed very soon.

Harold raised his hand to knock on his own front door and then changed his mind. He turned the handle and went in.

"I'm back!" His eyes went straight to the kitchen doorway at the far end of the hall, searching out Doreen. He almost tripped over the small boy playing at the foot of the stairs.

"Mam!" The boy was on his feet and backing down the hallway.

It had to be Stephen. Doreen had sent a couple of

photographs of their son over the years but they hadn't prepared him for this transformation from chubby toddler to schoolboy stranger.

"What is it?" called a female voice.

Harold's stomach tightened at the sound he hadn't heard for nearly six years.

"Mam! There's a man."

Harold moved further into the hall and crouched to Stephen's height. He reached out his hand to touch his son's hair. "It's alright, son. It's me, your dad."

But it wasn't alright – the boy's face blazed distrust. They were strangers. Stephen had been toddling when Harold marched away in September 1939. He was eight now with no memory of his father.

Doreen appeared, wiping her hands on her apron as she used to do when he came home from work. She was thinner than Harold remembered but still had that nervous habit of patting her hair to check it hadn't dropped its overnight curler-created shape. The prospect of this reunion had kept Harold alive. He'd used it to shut out the acrid smells and noise of the battlefield and then, later, the prison. He'd pictured swinging his wife around, kisses, laughter and young Stephen producing a ball for a kick about with his dad.

"Harold!"

He wasn't sure whether the expression on her face was horror or surprise. Then she took two steps forward and he felt her warm body once more in his arms.

"I'm glad to be back," he whispered into her hair.
"Me too."
"Mam!" Stephen pulled at his mother's skirt,

separating her from Harold.

Doreen made a pot of tea. Stephen sat beside his mother on the settee and Harold took the worn armchair under the resentful gaze of his son. Later they had sausage and mash, a ration book meal planned for two but now stretched to three. Stephen's eyes strayed covetously to Harold's plate and, ignoring the rumble in his own stomach, Harold chopped his sausage and pushed half of it onto his son's plate.

"Is there room on that settee for me?" Harold asked lightly when the washing up was done and Doreen had tuned to the new Light Program service on the wireless. "How about you sit on my knee, Stephen?"

Doreen shuffled to one side and Harold quickly squeezed onto the couch before Stephen could spread himself into the gap or move onto his mother's lap. Then he attempted to pull the boy into an embrace.

"Let go! You don't belong here. I want my mam!" The boy was all knees and elbows as he wrenched himself from Harold's clutches and into his mother's arms.

It felt like a knife was being slowly turned in Harold's heart. This wasn't the homecoming he'd played in his mind through the dark days of fighting and imprisonment. In his imagination Stephen had been overjoyed at his father's return.

"Take it slowly," Doreen said later when Stephen was in bed. "You're like a stranger stealing me away. Make friends with him."

The following day, when Harold came back from the Labour Exchange, his son was lying on the floor with a pile of matchsticks, a tube of glue, a crumpled picture torn from a magazine and a half-built model of a boat.

"That's top notch!" The scruffy model didn't deserve the excessive praise but Harold had to try. He sat down on the floor next to his son. "Which bit you working on next?"

The distrust was still there in the boy's eyes but he seemed more willing to talk. His words carried a hint of pride in what he'd accomplished so far. "The masts. They're the hardest 'cos they're so thin and spindly. Mam's got some rag I can use as sails."

When Stephen went to bed the model was left carefully propped on the rag rug. Doreen picked up her knitting and Harold got down on his knees and studied the creased photograph. Then he started laying out matchsticks and making joins with smears of glue. An hour later the main mast was complete and he carefully attached it to the ship.

"That should please him. I've done the most difficult bit."

Doreen looked up from her needles and wool. "I hope you're right," she said doubtfully. "He's very territorial, even with his school friends. He hates anyone touching his things."

The next morning Harold was finishing his porridge in the kitchen when he heard angry shouts and stamping feet from the other room. He rushed in to see Stephen draw back his leg and, with his booted foot, send the matchstick sailing ship crashing against the tiled hearth. It splintered into a wreck. "That was *my* model," the boy shrieked. "Not yours! You're not even a proper part of this family."

Then Stephen scarpered, slamming the front door and leaving Harold feeling as winded as if he'd been physically kicked by the little boy. For so long this homecoming and its associated feelings of love and happiness had been his goal. But now he missed the uncomplicated camaraderie of his fellow soldiers. His mates had understood the daily fear each of them lived with but Harold couldn't understand the outright rejection shown by his only child. When Doreen brought him a mug of tea he was sitting with his head in his hands.

"You can't recreate family bonds as quickly as the glue sets on those matches," she said quietly. She took his hand and squeezed it with affection. "It's the same with me and you. I'm so very glad you're back but we've been apart far longer than we were ever together. Having a man in the house again is going to take some getting used to. Fairy steps, we've all got to take fairy steps."

Fairy steps! What was Harold supposed to do in the meantime? Be always on his best behaviour like a guest in his own home? Coming back was difficult for him as well as them. In the army he'd had an important job fighting for his country as part of a team of great men. But returning soldiers were forced to take whatever work they could get, which at the moment wasn't a lot. Pre-war he'd been a skilled toolmaker, but the only work he could get on his visit to the Labour Exchange yesterday had been labouring for a building firm to clear bomb sites ready for the new pre-fabricated houses. It wasn't much for someone who'd put his life on the line for his country.

When he came home after his first day on the building site, he was exhausted and slumped into the armchair. A sullen looking Stephen was propelled in front of him by Doreen.

"Go on," Doreen prompted.

"I'm … sorry … about the model," Stephen whispered to his shoes. "Mr Armstrong from the ironmongers gave me more matches." A prod in the shoulder blades by his mother and he continued speaking. "We … could … work on it together, tonight."

Not tonight, please! Harold's back ached and his fingers were sore from heaving rubble. He wanted to doze not play daddy to a hostile child. But Doreen's eyes were boring into him, demanding the correct response. Like a clown he turned up the ends of his lips. He ruffled Stephen's hair. "Great, let's make a start before tea."

The reluctant boy didn't even try to mirror his dad's fake smile. Harold sensed it was going to be a painfully long evening. Stephen flattened out the creases in the magazine picture. They took half the damaged model each. It was mostly unsalvageable save for some of the matchsticks that could be carefully detached for reuse. Neither of them attempted conversation. Only the tick of the clock and the kitchen sounds of pots and pans measured the time until they'd be temporarily released from this unwanted bonding to eat.

"So how are the shipwrights doing?" Doreen asked cheerfully as she dished up potato and cheese bake. "Sorry, it's mostly potato."

Harold looked across at Stephen, giving him first chance to speak. For a brief second they made eye contact before Stephen looked away. Did that count as progress – his son looking him in the eye of his own free will instead of whispering forced words to his shoes?

"We're doing the groundwork first," Harold said. "Saving what can be saved before starting the build." He glanced at his son again but the boy was now fixed on his potato and cheese.

When Harold offered to wash up Stephen's face perked up. It fell again when Doreen brushed aside the offer of help.

"No," she said. "You two have important maritime matters to deal with. Off you go."

Sitting on the floor with a full stomach and tired muscles was uncomfortable and possibly pointless. Stephen spoke only when asked a direct question and answered in monosyllables. Surely it should be easier than this to gain acceptance by your own flesh and blood? It was a relief when Stephen went to bed and Harold could retire to the settee.

The next morning Harold was shaving at a mirror propped up on the windowsill above the kitchen sink. Stephen reached across to get a bowl from the draining board. For a couple of seconds their faces were reflected side by side. The father and son likeness between them was obvious. Stephen's nose, like Harold's, was slightly too large for his slim face and their chins both had the same square edge. Harold remembered one of the rare photos of himself at Stephen's age, taken just after his sick grandfather had moved in with them. Until then his granddad had been a shadowy figure working on the fishing boats and rarely at home. Granddad had shared Harold's bedroom and Harold had hated this intrusion and the attention his mother transferred from himself to her father. Granddad had tried hard to help by reading bedtime stories, making paper aeroplanes and giving the answers to the children's crossword in the evening newspaper. Resentful of the interloper, Harold had rejected it all.

Later Stephen was already engrossed in the boat when Harold got home from the building site.

"Be with you when I've had a wash," Harold called.

At the kitchen sink he caught sight of himself in the mirror again. His grandfather had never stopped trying and Harold had never stopped rebuffing him. He hadn't wanted an old man's help; he'd wanted the challenge of making his own aeroplanes, reading his own book and working out his own puzzle answers.

In the lounge the ship's hull was already well underway, slightly messy but recognisable. Harold wondered if Stephen had rushed it to get as much done as possible before his dad interfered. Doreen had got it wrong about father and son working on the ship together.

"You're a real craftsman with those matches," Harold said. "My basic skills are surplus to requirements, aren't they?"

Stephen glanced up at his dad. "I can do it myself."

"I can see that. You're doing good."

Stephen smiled proudly. "And Mam got sugar today. She's made a cake to celebrate you coming home."

"No eggs," Doreen said behind him. "But I've done my best."

She slipped her hand into his and he knew from her smile that she'd felt the upturn in Stephen's mood as well.

<u>Hit or Miss?</u>

Hit!

This story was published in *The People's Friend* in 2019 under the title 'Baby Steps'.

THE TRIP COLLECTOR

It was the Tuesday of the second week of the castle's winter opening hours. For the next six months visitors were welcome only at weekends and Stephen's bank balance would suffer. He didn't agree with barring the castle gates from Monday to Friday just because the weather had turned chilly. A cold breeze or a drop of rain never hurt anyone, so why must the castle tour guide shut up shop for five days each week? Plenty of older people enjoyed a mid-week break out of season and without the presence of running, ranting and roaring children. Stephen hated children; he had to charge them half price for the tour and then wear his saccharine sweet smile when their shouting and squawling drowned his commentary. At least, without children, winter working was peaceful, even if the pickings were poor.

Stephen's stories of Celts, cannons and courage barely covered his outgoings, despite his talents for acting, audience rapport and alliteration. This hand to mouth existence necessitated meticulous record keeping. Into the spreadsheet went his diminutive daily takings (minus the castle's colossal commission) and his expanding expenditure on rent, utilities and basic foodstuffs. If the difference between the two was positive, Stephen could sleep at night. This Tuesday he calculated his summer season surplus and halved it. Each half would fund a winter season journey and the first was scheduled for tomorrow.

All summer Stephen pined for the splendour of foreign lands. His pictures of palaces, people and paintings already sprawled over twenty-one albums. Each album covered a specific world zone and the zones were defined by Stephen's own classification system. He'd written to several glossy travel magazines about his system of dividing the world according to the number of worthwhile sites in an area rather than by continent or country. This meant that some zones consisted of only a couple of geographically small, but culturally well-endowed cities, such as Rome and Florence, whilst another zone contained the whole of Antarctica. None of the magazines had even printed the letter, never mind taken up his offer of a six-thousand-word article on the subject. Sometimes Stephen dwelt on those rejections and it dampened his re-telling of the castle's ghastly ghost story or diminished the twinkle in his eye and the strength of his handshake as he greeted tour guests.

Twice a year, once at the very beginning and once at the very end of the winter season, Stephen did his travelling and the spoils of each journey satisfied him for the next six months.

HIT OR MISS?

The first Biannual Trip (its importance created capital letters in his mind) of the winter season had been thoroughly planned and departure day was tomorrow. Stephen had a checklist to ensure his preparation left nothing to chance:

1. Make booking with travel agent. Jean was his favourite person to deal with. She remembered his gluten-free diet and advised on the availability of brochures. Some of the other staff thought he'd be happy with whatever they came up with. But Stephen liked to state a preference in advance. He'd tried using a local branch of the same travel firm but an equal breadth of options wasn't available, so now he only dealt with their flagship store which was a train ride away.
2. Buy extra pages for his loose-leaf scrap books. Where necessary he would also buy a new binder and create a second, third or even fourth volume for the required zone(s). This was where advance knowledge of what was available aided correct planning.
3. Research. A place couldn't be properly appreciated without knowing its history. That was why his castle tours got excellent reviews on TripAdvisor – he painted pictures with his narratives: images of the great kitchen in full swing with a turning spit dripping animal fat, contrasted with the siege of 1780 when food was so scarce they survived on stewed rat for a month. Internet research didn't cut the mustard; Stephen liked a physical guidebook, especially one from the library. Library

guidebooks didn't dent his finances and were often illegally annotated with previous travellers' tales and recommendations. He liked the sensation of holding a book that had escaped the confines of its small town home and travelled across the globe. Sometimes he thought he could smell garlic, spices and good coffee on the pages. He imagined the book being discussed, double-checked and used to discover new destinations over meals in tavernas, tiny cafés and tin shacks. Stephen held such books to his heart and dreamed.

4. Dog Care. Stephen had contemplated taking Theodore with him on the journey. As a retired greyhound he needed little exercise and was docile on the local bus. But it wasn't fair to inflict travel bustle, escalators and loudspeaker announcements on him. Imagine being a dog in a crowd and seeing only the legs and shoes of impatient strangers. To save Theodore's sanity, the dog sitter had to be booked and also paid to visit a week before the trip so Stephen could be assured that Theodore would settle with this rarely seen stranger.

5. Packing. Stephen couldn't understand people who hated packing and who fretted about forgetting something vital. Packing was part of the excitement. Packing had its own sub-checklist. His needs for the journey were simple:

Cheese and tomato sandwiches – there was no point in wasting a day's worth of tour guide tips on something dry and plastic-flavoured from the buffet trolley.

Phone – the ability to take selfie photographs was a boon to the solo traveller. It obviated the need to hijack a local and hope the chosen local wouldn't hijack the camera instead of capturing Stephen's smile.

Waterproof gear – winter season travelling meant being prepared for any eventuality.

As usual, the night before the trip Stephen barely slept. Mentally he flicked through his lists. Sandwiches wrapped in an old bread bag in the fridge. Train ticket pre-collected from the machine at the station and now in his wallet. Guide books already digested and placed in the rucksack to further peruse on the journey.

The next morning Stephen arrived at the station thirty minutes before departure and glanced at the board of lights to check his platform number.

CANCELLED. The word scorched his retinas. He scanned the list for later trains. CANCELLED. CANCELLED. The public address system broadcast a loud mumble about a signalling problem. Stephen's plans splintered. Empty album pages glared. A winter season of idleness and despair beckoned. A fog of panic made it difficult to think. He approached a man in uniform.

"Sorry, sir. Engineers are working on the issue. If you prefer not to wait you can claim a full refund online."

Stephen shook his head. He needed to make the trip. What would Jean do if he didn't stick to the itinerary they'd created together? Postponing would mean an extra dog-sitting fee that his expenditure spreadsheet wouldn't stand. He must travel today or wait six months until his next scheduled journey at the end of the winter season. For a while he stood like the post of a breakwater whilst an ocean of people ebbed and flowed around him. He wanted to cry but not here, not in public.

"Good news!" The return of the man in the uniform made Stephen jump. "There's a bus replacement service about to leave from the front of the station."

The threat of tears was gone. Stephen grabbed his rucksack and raced into the fresh air.

The bus ride felt like a wade through treacle and Stephen arrived at the travel agency two hours late. Jean waved and indicated she'd be with him when she'd finished with the couple already at her desk. Stephen found a seat and ate his sandwiches. He was washing them down with tea from his flask when Jean walked over with a cardboard box.

"Just as you requested - our old summer brochures focussing on the towns of the Rhine and the Danube. Enjoy!"

The tension of the morning had made him emotional. Stephen wanted to kiss her. A braver man wouldn't have hesitated but Stephen was no hero. Instead, he tentatively squeezed her hand as she put the box down. "Thank you, Jean," he said. "Very much. Being late, I was worried …"

His hand burned as he moved it away; he wasn't used to touching people.

"No problem." She patted him on the shoulder. She was still smiling; he hadn't overstepped the mark with physical contact.

Stephen decanted the brochures into his rucksack, his heart soaring at the prospect of a winter spent clipping, sticking and imagining the journeys he could make if money was plentiful. Jean produced fresh tea and two slices of cake sandwiched with jam. He glanced at her, his hand hovering over the Victoria sponge.

"Yes, gluten-free," she whispered.

The words squeezed at Stephen's heart. His mother was the only other person who remembered. They remained on the chairs meant for customers who were waiting to see an advisor. Jean told him that river cruises were now the thing. Stephen told her shops didn't stock photographic corners anymore and he had to buy online because using glue didn't look good. He glanced at his watch and noted sadly that the dog sitter would be into overtime. When he said goodbye to Jean, he didn't have the courage to touch her hand again. He hoped she wouldn't retire before he journeyed here again in the spring.

The return replacement bus was hindered by rush hour traffic and the spray from a sudden downpour of rain. Stephen was impervious to the gloom. He focused on the wonderful winter in front of him. When the albums were finished, he planned to finally create that talk for the plentiful, paying punters of clubs across the region, "Journeys from My Armchair."

Hit or Miss?

Miss.

'The Trip Collector' failed to make the grade in three competitions during 2020: The Broadway Arts Festival, The Costa Short Story Award and a competition organised by author Louise Beech to celebrate her fiftieth birthday. However, I grew fond of Stephen and wanted him to have his fifteen minutes of fame in this book.

COFFEE CAPERS

Pete's brain buzzed with the names of the different coffees: cappuccino, frappe, macchiato, cortado and more. He'd had a go at most of them on the training course but, like French lessons at school, he feared it might be a case of in one ear and out the other. Hopefully, the customers and staff of the Copacabana Coffee Shop would be forgiving towards him.

The large sign on the shop front was still blank but a sheet of A4 paper stuck in the window proclaimed that the café was now open for business. It was part of a chain of coffee shops expanding across the country and providing work for people like Pete.

There were double yellow lines outside so he was forced to park a hundred yards down the road where there were no restrictions. He jogged back up to the shop, anxious not to be late on his first day. Trainee positions were like gold dust and he didn't want to mess things up. He'd started last week with five days of training at head office, today would be his first real work experience.

"I'll be calling in mid-morning on your first day," his tutor had said the previous Friday when they'd parted company. He'd consulted the schedule on the computer screen. "I'll see you at the branch in Little Chapworth. It opened last week but things are behind schedule so it might be a bit manic. Once everything's sorted there, you'll go on to Hulmington which is due to open in a fortnight - assuming your work is up to scratch."

Pete was worried he wouldn't be up to the job. Until last week he never knew there were so many different ways of serving coffee and the names of the drinks looked like a foreign language to him. Today he was going to do his absolute best to get it right. Pete took the rucksack off his back and pushed open the café door with his shoulder. A small queue of people stood alongside the counter. The air was thick with the smell of freshly brewed coffee and the gentle burbling, whistling and banging noises of the coffee machine. Snatches of conversation drifted around as customers debated the merits of Danish pastries and fresh porridge to accompany their breakfast coffee.

Pete slipped off his jacket and straightened his new, work-issued, navy polo shirt. The company logo was embroidered in gold on the left breast. The barista at the till waved him over as soon as she saw the familiar uniform.

"Pete Sugden." He introduced himself and held out his hand. "I think you're expecting me."

"Wonderful! You're a sight for sore eyes. I'm Sonia, the manager." She shook his hand enthusiastically. "We've been open a week but unfortunately things are still only half-finished in here." She gestured at the bulbs hanging from the ceiling without shades, the large blank board headed 'Menu' hanging behind the counter and a stack of paintings leaning against the wall which were obviously waiting to be hung.

"Thank goodness the customers don't seem to mind. We're the only café in the High Street and business has been good. And once you get stuck in as well it will make things easier for us all." Sonia nodded towards the other barista who was patiently explaining the invisible menu to a young mum with a toddler in a pushchair. "It's taking us so long to serve people at the moment."

"And all coffees come in three sizes," the barista finished triumphantly as though she'd just finished a long poem she'd learned by heart.

"Sorry," said the young mum, "what flavour syrups did you say you had?"

The barista took a deep breath and started again.

"Most of the customers are understanding but some of them do get impatient." Sonia handed Pete a sheet of A4 paper. "This is everything we serve, along with all the prices. It's pretty standard coffee shop fare; let me know if anything doesn't make sense. But we're all trying to share that one menu, so don't keep it to yourself!"

Pete took the sheet of paper, put on the large apron issued to him during the training course and slipped behind the counter. There wasn't a lot of room for manoeuvre. He, Sonia and the second barista were all fighting for space but eventually they figured out a way of making it work.

Pete looked down at the A4 sheet; some of these were going to be easier to manage than others. He and the other trainees had practised the basic menu components the previous week. The 'Pot of Tea for One' and the 'Flat White' were easy. Latte was straight forward too but Cappuccino still caused him problems - he'd have to refer to the menu to get that one correct. He wondered if any of the customers would realise if things weren't quite right.

The barista next to him was sprinkling cocoa powder through a stencil on to a hot drink. It required a firm hand to ensure the powder came out at a steady rate rather than in a big rush. The barista removed the stencil to reveal a perfect heart shape. Pete gave a little round of applause. The manager frowned at him and indicated he should concentrate on his own work.

"Babychoccino, iced latte, espresso," he muttered the three drinks over and over to himself to keep them in his brain - it annoyed the others if he kept asking for the menu to check what came next.

"One large skinny latte and an iced espresso, please."

The customer had a loud voice and it cut straight into Pete's thoughts making him lose track of what he was doing. He was halfway through 'Babychoccino' and didn't know how to finish it off. He looked at what he had in front of him. It gave him no hint of how to proceed. He needed the menu but that was with Sonia by the till and she was discussing it with a customer.

He glanced over his shoulder and discovered that the queue of customers was watching him. His face burned. He felt like an actor on stage and he began to tremble. The second barista was trying to clarify with the customer whether the drinks were to take away or drink in. She had to ask the question three times before the customer took his eyes off Pete and answered. Then the customer stared straight back at Pete again.

Pete felt wobbly now.

"That man's going to fall!" A little girl's voice rang out across the café.

Pete swayed in his elevated position above the counter. He got a grip on himself and tried to visualise the A4 menu and how to finish 'Babychoccino'. He raised his hand to put the final touch, hoping that somehow it might intuitively come to him. It didn't so he made a guess.

"That's wrong!"

The voice of his signwriting tutor made Pete jump. He dropped his paintbrush and clung to the stepladder to avoid toppling onto the cake counter.

"It's an 'O' not an 'A' at the end of 'Babychoccino'," said his tutor.

Hit or Miss?

Hit!

This story was published in *The Weekly News* in 2018. It is a reflection of my love of writing in coffee shops. Or, possibly, not actually writing but staring, eavesdropping and letting my mind conjure up stories about the people around me.

TRAVELLING WITH TIM

"Welcome to the honeymoon suite!" Mark swept me into his arms and staggered over the threshold of our New York hotel room.

"Put me down!"

Grinning, my new husband dropped me onto the king-sized bed and rubbed his back exaggeratedly. "Lucky I did that extra weight training at the gym!"

I punched him playfully. Mark popped the cork from a bottle of champagne and handed me a glass. The bubbles danced up my nose and I leant over to kiss my new spouse. He responded more passionately but I pulled away.

"No time for that," I said. "We'll miss our evening river cruise."

This planned excursion was important. I had a date to keep with my first husband on that boat.

"It's Tim, isn't it?" A cloud passed over Mark's

face. "It will be a clean break this time?"

I nodded and swallowed the lump in my throat. It was going to be hard saying goodbye for the last time and I hoped I wouldn't lose my nerve out on the river.

The temperature dropped as the boat pulled away from the quayside and the wind tossed spray into my eyes. I snuggled into Mark's strong arms and listened to the commentary. From the water Manhattan was a kaleidoscope of electric colour that my camera could only capture as blurred blobs. We chugged past skyscrapers, old factories and on towards the statue of Liberty.

Liberty, freedom – that's what Tim and I needed now. I had managed to move on and it was time for Tim to do the same. I glanced at my watch and my heart began to thump.

"Mark, I'd love a hot chocolate." I had to be alone. I didn't want to introduce Tim to Mark; they'd never met and it was better kept that way.

My husband's eyes met mine with a knowing look then he released me from his arms and headed towards the refreshment stand. I scanned the throng of chattering tourists and then squeezed my way up to the deck railings.

Tim and Mark were like chalk and cheese. Tim was impulsive, a 'seize the moment' type but Mark considers things before acting. He would never have rushed across a busy road to present me with flowers like Tim did.

But my marriage to Tim lasted only two years and I didn't see the end coming. It knocked me for six. After three months my sister had dragged me from my pit of despair and forced me onto a weekend break in Prague. I went reluctantly. Tim loved travelling and we'd been working our way through our own list of 'places to see before we have children'. New York was to have been our next trip. It was all planned but when going there together was no longer an option it lost its attraction and the holiday was cancelled.

Prague began my journey back to life. The bustling anonymity of Charles' Bridge made me realise that whatever I did, the world continued. My sister sensed my improving mood.

"When you get home why not get yourself back into circulation?" she asked gently. "There's plenty more fish in the sea. Don't let losing Tim ruin your life."

I felt as though she'd slapped me in the face. "We were married. I can't pretend it never happened."

But travelling gave me my confidence back. I booked a solo trip to Paris, where Tim had proposed and I retraced that evening by taking a boat trip down the Seine. Each time I put a ghost to rest or did something without him it got slightly easier but I knew at some point we'd have to have a final showdown.

I visited the Nile and the Rhine. River trips were like a magnet to me. It was soothing to stand on deck watching the water and listening to the gentle chug of the engines. In the meantime, I met Mark and did something I never thought possible: I fell in love again and my broken heart began to heal. When Mark proposed I accepted.

"Let's honeymoon in New York!" Mark's eyes had danced with enthusiasm.

I immediately thought of Tim and the trip we'd

been planning together. Guilt wrapped itself around me. How could I honeymoon with Mark in a place I'd talked so much about with Tim?

"You have to let go of Tim," my sister had said when we discussed it. "It's unfair to Mark to have Tim constantly haunting your relationship. New York will put a final end to it."

It was arranged Tim and I would say our final goodbyes on the Hudson River.

Mark knew about this third person on our honeymoon and I think he understood why. But now, here I was alone for the last time with my first love. I didn't want to lose him but I had to let go completely if I was to live my life. I'd already left part of him in Prague, Paris and Germany.

Turning my back to the river and wind, I retrieved the brown, opaque container from my voluminous handbag and ran my fingers over the label indicating that the contents were 'the cremated remains of Timothy John McDonald'.

"Thank you for everything." I whispered and kissed the urn. "We had a wonderful time together. Enjoy yourself until we meet again."

I started to unscrew the lid but my fingers were cold and clumsy. The complete casket spun off the rail and into the river. The lump in my throat grew huge and the tears in my eyes weren't caused by the biting wind.

There was a tap on my shoulder and I turned to look into the loving face of my new husband. He kissed me and handed me a mug of hot chocolate decorated with cream.

I had a feeling that Tim would have given us his blessing.

Hit or Miss?

Miss.

'Travelling with Tim' failed to hit the mark in a competition organised by *Best* magazine in 2011. I didn't submit to the other women's magazines because I felt the subject matter wasn't quite suitable.

NIGHT LIFE

George didn't take long to acclimatise to being awake at night and spending his days asleep in the hostel. He enjoyed walking back from work under the stars, with the sky hinting at the red dawn to come. He marvelled at how warm it still was and wondered when the weather would finally break. It made sense to sleep during the day when the sun was too hot and the crowds were swarming.

Bournemouth was enjoying a summer like 1976 and the nights were sticky with a heat that had spent the day burning bare skin and melting ice cream. The town's cash registers were bursting with the extravagance of day trippers and holidaymakers. Businesses were desperate for casual workers to meet the surge in demand. There were handwritten 'staff needed' signs in almost all the shops and pubs.

The *Corfu Kebab Shop* had employed George to cover the late shift from 10pm to 4am, paying him cash in hand, no questions asked, no references required. It was probably illegal but it suited George. The kebab customers were high on sun and drink and took no notice of the unshaven, tired-looking man with the scar on his cheek who served them. They were too self-absorbed to link him with the smooth-faced school teacher in a suit and tie pictured in the national newspapers.

It was an old photo of a slimmer, happier George. He'd forgotten the picture existed. The police must have got it from school. George had had the foresight to remove all the photographs at home before he left Newcastle. They'd gone in a black bag to the tip. A more recent image in the press would have made his disappearance harder to pull off.

Samantha had been the photographer in their relationship. She'd taken pictures of him and his grin in Rome, Paris and New York. Right now, the police should think he was travelling again - thanks to cousin Hank in Toronto. He was using George's credit card to do his shopping. George had heard that tip on the radio. The presenter had been interviewing someone in the States who ran a business helping people to disappear. The important thing was to set a false trail. To do this George had sent a credit card to Toronto with a fabricated story for Hank about debt and needing to evade his creditors. Soon, he'd tell his cousin the heat was off and he could stop spending. Then George would send his other card to an old Spanish exchange partner who now lived in Brazil. There were giant holes in his disappearance attempt, George knew, but he was doing his best to distance himself from what had happened at home. He wanted the authorities to think it had happened in his absence

– a random attack on an innocent woman.

The police were using social media and newspapers in an attempt to locate George who, they said, was out of the country and unaware of the tragic death of his wife. So far no one had reported a sighting of him. The big problem would come when the new school term started in September and he was expected back at work. He needed to return as a newly grieving widower, without any shadow of suspicion over his character. But before that, on his way home from work tonight, George was going to fulfil a promise made to Samantha more than a quarter of a century ago.

He scanned the buildings to his left and right. They were peppered with 'No Vacancies' signs and tourist board rosettes. Cars with roof boxes were parked nose to tail along the kerb. Buckets and spades stood sentry for the night outside front doors.

George spotted the name he was looking for above the bay window of a beige building to his right: The White Bull Hotel.

A jumble of images tumbled into his mind. Samantha in her scarlet going-away dress as they booked in at reception. Samantha emerging from the en suite bathroom in a flimsy peach negligee and a cloud of flowery perfume. He remembered the way the breakfast waiter had given him an extra rasher each morning.

"Got to keep your strength up, sir," the man had said with a suggestive wink and a nudge.

George and Samantha had spent seven blissful nights at the White Bull Hotel, twenty-six years ago. Now he'd returned to Bournemouth alone and Samantha was dead.

He wondered if the hotel still had the same fluffy towels that they'd wrapped themselves in after showering sand from between their toes and sun lotion from their bodies. Perhaps their names were in an old register, filed away somewhere in the hotel cellar - ghostly signatures from a perfect time.

"I love it here," Samantha had said, as they feasted on their last Full English before leaving for the train station. "Promise you'll bring me back?"

"I promise," he'd said, meaning it.

That's when the photographer had captured them in a split-second flash. They were staring adoringly at one another. The hotel had asked permission and then included it in a new promotional leaflet. Samantha had loved their little taste of fame. For several months the leaflet had had a prominent place on their second-hand coffee table.

He never brought Samantha back to the White Bull. In the intervening years she'd got a taste for sightseeing holidays abroad and lately, as things between them had deteriorated, they hadn't gone anywhere. But now he'd come back to keep his promise of a return trip, fuelled by his guilty conscience and the memories of earlier, happier days. Once upon a time he and Samantha had been good together, before something had soured inside her and she'd started to hate him. Now he wanted to make amends to the woman he'd once loved. George touched the scar on his cheek and wondered what had warped her mind and turned her against him.

Very few of The White Bull's windows were still illuminated this late at night. He fingered the plastic freezer bag in his pocket. It contained Samantha's wedding ring and the locket that she always wore.

He'd given it to her on their first wedding anniversary.

"I've put photos in of us on our honeymoon," he'd said, opening it up. He'd been a softie back then.

When her parents died a couple of years ago, he and Samantha were arguing a lot. She told him her mum and dad were going in the locket instead.

"At least they always loved me!" she'd said in her usual over dramatic way.

He never bothered to look which pictures of them she'd chosen.

Now he scanned the front door of the hotel for a letter box. What would the hotel staff do with the jewellery? Sell it cheaply for cash or donate it to charity? Either way they wouldn't know it had been pulled from a corpse and he would have fulfilled his promise – even if it wasn't his actual wife he was bringing back here, only her jewellery.

Samantha had only been dead a few minutes when he'd decided to stage his disappearance and take what he could of her back to their honeymoon hotel. He was a well-built man and the police wouldn't believe he'd acted in self-defence. Samantha had verbally and mentally abused him for years and he could put up with that.

"The way you leer at other women is ridiculous," she'd hiss at him if he'd passed the time of day with a waitress or female shop assistant. "As if they'd be interested in an excuse for a man like you!"

Recently the abuse had become physical. She'd started attacking him with her stilettos and long finger nails. Her talons had caused the scar on his cheek. The slightest thing provoked her, like him forgetting to buy milk on the way home. On that last night he'd mentioned a new shirt he'd bought.

"A waste of money!" she'd screamed. "You never look good in anything!"

Then she'd lunged towards him with the kitchen knife. He'd been hanging a picture and the hammer was still in his hand. Without thinking he'd brought it down on top of her head to stop the knife making contact with his chest.

Now the freezer bag slipped silently through the letter box of The White Bull and George disappeared into the darkness.

The following lunchtime uniformed police woke him in his bunk. He was barely allowed the time to pull on jeans and a T-shirt before they took him from the hostel in handcuffs.

"The hotel receptionist matched the photos in the locket to the old sales brochure displayed in reception," the detective inspector explained in the interview room. "She wanted to contact you in case the jewellery had been stolen. She found your name and address in their archived files and the clever girl put two and two together and realised you were the man in the newspapers. Uniform have been knocking door to door all morning. The hostel manager remembered your Geordie accent and it was easy from there. Now, tell us about the murder of your wife."

"Are you saying my wife is dead?" George tried to morph his voice into a shocked, innocent whisper but fury at his wife made it impossible. Why hadn't Samantha switched the photos in the locket as she'd threatened? Why hadn't he checked?

Even after her death she was still manipulating his life.

Hit or Miss?

Miss.

Night Life didn't make the grade in three competitions between 2013 and 2017 and was also rejected by *The Weekly News*. Its initial inspiration came from a competition asking for stories to be based around a seaside hotel.

CASUALTY

Brian was uncomfortable lying on his back on the tarmac. It had rained earlier and the dampness was seeping into his jeans and hoody. His leg was at an awkward angle and almost numb. The dark red stain on the denim around his thigh didn't look good.

The fire engine had just arrived but there was still no sign of an ambulance. One of the brown-clad fire officers jumped from the cab and gave him a cursory check-over.

"Did you lose consciousness when the car hit you?" the fireman asked.

"No."

"Any double-vision or nausea?"

"No. It's just the blood." Brian indicated his ripped jeans and the large red stain that had soaked the fabric. "I'm worried about my leg. I can hardly feel it."

"Stay calm. The ambulance will be here soon."

"Over here!" Another fireman was calling and gesticulating at his colleagues. "Unconscious pregnant woman trapped in the car!"

"I'm needed. Lie still until the medics get here."

Brian knew that Paula was the woman in the car. Paula was his wife. Twenty minutes ago they'd been drinking coffee together. She'd stroked the bump beneath her T-shirt.

"It's hard to imagine us being parents."

Brian knew what she meant. They were both thirty but still leading a nomadic, student-like existence. Their career choice was the main barrier to them having a permanent home and a secure future. London seemed full of people like them, all fighting over the same few casual jobs to tide them over until that big break came along.

Sometimes Brian got work as an extra in one of the soaps. He'd travel up to Manchester and put his heart and soul into downing a pint in the Rovers Return, hoping that one of the producers would spot him and offer him a proper role. He was always disappointed and, to make it worse, the pints weren't even real. They were very weak shandy, watered down with lemonade and too sweet for Brian's taste.

Now he could hear the ambulance siren. The temptation to lever himself up onto his elbows and wave the crew over was strong. He was desperate to be rescued from his cold, uncomfortable position on the road. But the medics would prioritise and Paula, with her bump, would be way ahead of him in the list.

He'd met Paula at drama school. Initially they'd been just mates. Each had given the other a shoulder to cry on after a failed audition. Then they'd both submitted showreels for a new children's TV program looking for presenters. And they'd both been invited for a screen test. Neither of them was successful and they spent the evening commiserating in the pub. After that they'd become an item and shared a grotty bedsit.

"Pregnant woman, unconscious, suspected fractured pelvis." One of the firefighters was briefing the ambulance crew. "We're going to have to use the cutting gear."

Brian turned his head towards the car. 'Cutting gear' sounded risky. Paula had only come today to keep him company. He'd never forgive himself if she got hurt by that giant tin-opener.

"Do we know the lady's name?" one of the ambulance crew called.

There was a general shaking of heads.

"Paula." Brian was surprised at how weak his voice sounded; it was difficult to project when he was prone on the floor with his head back. "She's called Paula. And be careful, that equipment looks lethal. I hope you're not novices."

"We know what we're doing. Is she a mate of yours?"

"She's my wife."

"He's in the way," declared one of the firefighters. He was pacing around the car whilst the others were preparing to open it up like a giant can of beans. "We'll have to move him."

A stretcher was produced from the back of the ambulance. Someone fitted Brian with a neck brace. On the count of three they lifted him onto the stretcher and moved him to the grass verge.

"Any chance of a drink?" Brian asked, running his tongue around his dry mouth.

"No." The paramedic was firm. "That leg doesn't look good. It might be fractured, if it is you'll be taken straight into surgery."

Brian lifted his arm and indicated the ambulance. "Can't you take me to hospital now?" The stretcher and grass verge were an improvement on the tarmac but the sun was setting and he was beginning to shiver.

"Sorry but as soon as your wife is cut free, she'll be in that vehicle. She and her unborn baby are our priority." The ambulance man fetched a red blanket from the ambulance and tucked it round Brian. "It shouldn't take too long."

Last year Paula had a got a job on a shopping channel demonstrating mail order costume jewellery. It paid proper money and now they were saving for the deposit on a flat. But, with Brian having no regular work, a baby was still out of the question.

The noise of the cutting gear tore through his brain. Poor Paula, it must be deafening inside the car. Brian wondered if she was thirsty like him. They'd been called away before finishing their coffees at the refreshment caravan earlier. Paula had got in the car and he'd walked across the road in front of her. The van on the opposite carriageway had supposedly lost control and caused the accident. From his prone position, Brian couldn't see what was happening with that driver and his passengers. He wondered if they were walking wounded.

The noise of the cutting gear stopped and there was a sudden eerie silence around the accident scene. Brian began to feel panicky. The emergency crews were huddled together, presumably planning their next move. But why weren't they lifting Paula out of the car?

If only she would give him a wave to show that she was alright.

"The baby's in danger...labour..." Snatches of conversation became audible as the group broke up. "...risk of maternal death..."

Brian gave a quick glance around to see if anyone was watching him and then sat up. He craned his neck to try and get a glimpse of his wife. Only the top of her head was visible. He moved his cold, numb leg and wondered about standing up.

"Let's get her out. Someone radio ahead to the labour ward."

Then the firemen and paramedics were once more around the car like bees on a honeypot. Within a minute Paula appeared strapped to a board. Her bump looked skew-whiff as it was silhouetted against the setting sun. Her eyes were closed but she gave the rotund padding a shove, as though stopping it from escaping from under her T-shirt.

Brian grinned; all was well.

Then the director of the Volunteer Casualty Simulation Group appeared at his side and pushed him back down into a prone position on the stretcher. "Let's keep things realistic, shall we?"

Brian started moaning as though his leg had really been broken by a collision with a car. He wasn't being paid for today's role helping to train the emergency services but there could be a TV producer around here somewhere.

Hit or Miss?

Hit!

'Casualty' was published in *The Weekly News* in 2015. The inspiration for this story came from a newspaper article about volunteers who happily give their time as 'pretend casualties' so the emergency services can stage mock disasters.

CLOTHES TO DIE FOR

Jackie knocked on the office door and breathed deeply. Her palms were sweaty and the words of her planned speech swirled in her head. Would Miss Riley think the coloured designs she'd sketched silly and send her away with a flea in her ear?

At school Jackie had dreamed of becoming a fashion designer like Mary Quant. She'd imagined Twiggy strutting the catwalk wearing *her* designs. Jackie's teacher had written a glowing reference for her art college application and she'd been called for an interview. But her father had stopped everything.

'Drawing pictures of dresses isn't a proper job,' he'd said. 'A vicar's daughter shouldn't encourage women to bare their legs in these new miniskirts – it's not right.'

'Learn shorthand and typing instead,' her mother suggested brightly.

'But I want to be creative!' Jackie fought back the

tears as her dreams were trampled.

Her father fiddled with his clerical collar. 'You could be a seamstress at Aldgate's. Miss Riley mentioned one of the girls was leaving to get wed. I'll ask for you.'

'That's not the sort of creative I mean.' The sewing room at Aldgate's would be full of mournful matrons, uninterested in fashion, pop music or men. The atmosphere would be quiet and respectful.

Her mother had patted her arm. 'It's only until you find a fiancé.'

The week after she finished school, Jackie had started work at Aldgate's under the watchful eye of Miss Riley. She'd struggled to sew in a straight line and keep to the prescribed seam allowance. She had to ask for help as the cream fabric rucked up around the sewing machine needle.

'It's the tension,' one of her new workmates explained with a smile. 'If it's too tight or too slack everything goes haywire!'

Eventually Jackie got the knack and also got to know the other machinists, who were younger and merrier than she'd expected. The wireless played the Beatles and Elvis while the girls twirled around the room during their tea breaks. Aldgate's sewing room was a happy place but Jackie still wanted to design and she began using her new sewing skills to make her own clothes at home.

'I knew you'd settle,' Jackie's mother said. 'Aldgate's is a good place for clergy family to work.'

'And speaking of clergy,' her father said. 'George, the new curate's coming for tea tomorrow. He's a decent man. You'll like each other.'

Now, waiting nervously for Miss Riley to answer

her knock, Jackie smoothed her short shift dress. It was one of her own creations, chosen carefully for today's meeting. Patterned with blue swirls, the dress was modern without being outrageous.

She'd worn it when George came to tea. Her father would have forbidden anything shorter or the hot-pants she'd made. Amazingly, the new curate had turned out to be tall, dark and handsome. Despite his clerical collar and shirt Jackie could see he was broad-shouldered and gorgeous. When he complimented her on her dress, she blushed.

'I'd love to see you again,' George said, when her parents left the room with the dirty crockery. 'Are you free on Saturday?'

Jackie hesitated. The kitchen door was open and her parents would be listening. If George had been in any other profession, she would have accepted immediately but, coming from a clergy family, she knew the restrictions being a vicar's wife might impose. George's invitation was far from a marriage proposal, but Jackie took the long view; it was pointless wasting time on someone who couldn't offer the future she wanted, no matter how good looking he was. Jackie had watched her mother live in the shadow of a parish priest, baking for fetes, making tea after services, hosting meetings and welcoming all and sundry into her home whether it was convenient or not. Jackie didn't want that, she still wanted to become a fashion designer, a woman with her own career.

'Yes, she's free.' Jackie's father returned with a fresh pot of tea.

Jackie couldn't contradict him; it would be impolite.

'Great.' George grinned. 'I've got two tickets for the Blues match. Will you come?'

Her father was looking pleased. There was no point making excuses. She nodded mutely.

The following Saturday she wore a thick sweater and trousers against the cold.

'The Blues were one of the reasons I chose this parish,' George explained as they found a place to stand on the terraces. 'I've supported them since I was a boy.'

As the ground became crowded George and Jackie were forced closer together and he held her hand. Jackie's stomach somersaulted at the touch of his skin. She looked up at him and saw he'd felt the electricity too. How she wished he wasn't a clergyman.

'George! Good to see you!' A middle-aged man was patting the curate on the back and pumping his hand.

George introduced them. 'Jackie, this is Rodney from the Men's Group at the church and these are his sons.'

Jackie shook hands with Rodney and nodded at the three gawky teenagers.

Once the match got underway it was impossible to talk. The shouting was deafening and the thunderous wooden rattles made her jump. It was hard to concentrate on the twenty-two men running around the pitch as she was squashed from all sides.

George must have sensed her discomfort. 'Sorry, football's not really a ladies' pastime, is it?' he said as they left the ground. 'I should have been more considerate. Will you give me another chance next week? But you choose where we go.'

This was Jackie's opportunity to explain she didn't want to see him again but he was still holding her hand and sending tiny electric shocks through her body. He was grinning and his eyes were flirting with her. Her heart ignored her head.

'Let's go to the Zodiac coffee bar.' The Zodiac was where the 'in crowd' went and Jackie had never been. 'But you won't wear your dog collar, will you?'

George had laughed and given his word.

Jackie moved closer to the frosted glass of the office door and listened. Perhaps Miss Riley hadn't heard the first knock. Miss Riley's voice was speaking and then there was a long pause before she spoke again. She must be on the telephone. It wouldn't do Jackie's case any good if she interrupted something important. She stood quietly at the door for a bit longer.

In the days leading up to the Zodiac date Jackie had begged advice from her workmates on what to drink and what to put on the juke box. Espresso frothy coffee and 'Love Me Do' got the majority vote. Then she spent hours deciding what to wear before choosing red Capri pants with a white blouse.

George telephoned the vicarage just before they were due to meet. 'I'm sorry, Jackie, I can't go to the Zodiac. Rodney's had a heart attack.' His voice was emotional. 'The family needs comforting and help to arrange the funeral. But I'll come to see you this evening. I promise.'

Jackie felt sorry for Rodney's family but this was exactly what she'd feared would happen if she got involved with a clergyman. A vicar's wife and family always took second place to the parishioners. She changed out of the Capri pants and instead spent the afternoon sketching blouses and wondering if she'd ever get a foothold in the design world.

George looked drained when he arrived. 'It's worse when you know someone personally, like I did Rodney. His daughter was knitting a new Blues scarf. She said her dad couldn't be buried with his old one because it was full of holes.'

'How was his wife?'

'Devastated. And she was upset that the funeral director could only offer cream or white shrouds. She said they stole her husband's personality. He was a lively man and football mad. I said I'd look into an alternative. Can Aldgate's offer anything?'

Jackie shook her head, thinking of the hundreds of plain, light-coloured shrouds that passed through the sewing-room every week. She felt upset for this unknown widow and sorry that her work at the factory didn't please everyone.

When George left, Jackie took out her sketch pad and coloured pencils again. She tore up the afternoon's blouses and started afresh. Her brain was buzzing with a new idea. Art college wasn't going to happen but perhaps Jackie could still make her mark in the design world.

'What do you think?' Nervously Jackie showed George one of her designs after church the following day.

This wasn't just a test of her creative ability; it was a test of George's attitude to a woman with ambition. Would he back her ideas and, therefore, her career or would he encourage her to be the little woman at home?

He studied the sheet of paper for some time. 'The colours aren't quite right but that's easily corrected.

And, not everybody will approve, people will either love them or loathe them.'

'So do you think I should submit them to Aldgate's management?'

'Absolutely.'

Joyfully, Jackie had stood on tip-toe and kissed him on the cheek. For a second George had looked shocked and then he'd pulled her close and kissed her properly for the first time.

'Come in!' called Miss Riley through the frosted office door at the same moment that Thomas Aldgate, managing director of Aldgate's Coffin Furniture, appeared at Jackie's side.

'I understand you've got something for us,' he said as they settled themselves around a scratched wooden table in Miss Riley's office.

'I … yes.' Jackie stumbled over her words - she hadn't expected Mr Aldgate to be there. 'Not all men are suited to a plain white shroud.' She explained about Rodney and then with shaking hands laid her sketches on the table. 'So, I've designed some new shrouds using the colours of local football teams.'

A silence followed and Jackie didn't know where to look or what to say. The designs were obviously inappropriate. She'd overstepped the mark for a mere machinist.

'This is a brilliant idea!' Mr Aldgate spoke after what seemed like an age.

'You really think so?'

'Definitely. Miss Riley, please advertise for a new junior machinist. Jackie will be busy bringing these designs to life.'

Back at her sewing machine Jackie trembled with excitement. George had encouraged her with the designs and she couldn't wait to tell him the good news. If he was still pleased then maybe a future together was possible.

She ran to meet him after work. 'Mr Aldgate saw my sketches. I'm going to be a designer!'

George whooped and twirled her around. 'I still owe you that visit to the Zodiac,' he said. 'Let's celebrate there and plan your new career.'

Jackie beamed. Her ambition and George's clergyman vocation could exist side by side.

Hit or Miss?

Miss.

Between 2015 and 2021 this story was rejected by *Woman's Weekly*, *My Weekly* and *Woman's Own*. It was a near miss with *The People's Friend* who asked for some editorial changes before eventually rejecting it because they thought the content too dark (I should have learned my lesson after the failure of the earlier story, 'Travelling with Tim'). 'Clothes to Die For' also failed to make the grade in three competitions. This is one of my favourite stories which is why I kept plugging away at it. It was inspired by a visit to the Coffin Works in Birmingham.

MAN VERSUS MACHINE

The reception area at Perfect Bodies Gym was decorated with posters of toned, muscled bodies working out. Alan gazed at these images of perfection and his heart thumped with nerves. His workmates had already told him Perfect Bodies Gym was a cut above most of the fitness centres in the area.

"It's full of well-honed bodies belonging to well-heeled people," his boss had said. "They have high standards and expect everyone to work hard. Don't let the side down."

"On the rewards side, their coffee is good!" added one of the other engineers. "It almost compensates for their slave-driver regime."

Coffee was the last thing Alan wanted. Caffeine would increase his heart rate further. The bottle of water in his kit bag would keep him hydrated.

The receptionist flashed Alan a perfect white smile. Her arms, visible beneath the short sleeves of her uniform blouse, were toned and tanned. Her light brown hair was cropped short and streaked with blonde. Her name badge said, 'Suzanne'.

"Is it your first visit?" she asked.

Alan nodded, too much in awe to speak.

"Follow me," Suzanne instructed.

Several people in immaculate exercise gear passed them as Suzanne led the way along a corridor and up a flight of stairs. Alan looked down at his own training shoes, the white bits had gone grey and they were scuffed along the toes. Suzanne was staring at his well-worn footwear too and his cheeks burned with shame.

The gym floor was crowded.

"Unfortunately, this is one of our busiest times," Suzanne said. "People like to come straight after work. It would have helped if you could have got here earlier." She left the rebuke hanging in the air.

"Sorry," Alan apologised. "I got held up at the office, paperwork and stuff, and then the traffic was bad."

"All the cardio equipment is in this area." Suzanne opened her arms wide to indicate the rows of treadmills, cross-trainers, bikes and rowing machines. "Where would you like to start?"

"This is the program I've been given." Alan handed her a sheet of paper. Against each machine was a target duration time. "Does it matter which order I do them in?"

Suzanne ran her finger down the sheet. Around them feet pounded, people panted and music played with a thudding beat.

"The treadmill is a priority." Suzanne pointed towards an empty machine.

MAN VERSUS MACHINE

Alan's heart sank. The treadmill was the most difficult of all the cardio machines. He'd hoped to begin with something less challenging. The cross-trainers and rowing-machines didn't cause him half as many problems. He'd been a regular at the gym round the corner from the office until it went bankrupt. There he'd always managed to leave the treadmill until last, by which point he was warmed up and in the swing of things.

Suzanne left him to it. Alan stowed his kit bag to the left of the machine and glanced around nervously to check if anyone was watching him. The man on the treadmill to his right was sprinting like Usain Bolt and he had the muscled body to match. The woman on his left was obviously a gym bunny. Her designer vest and shorts emphasised her flat stomach and firm limbs.

Alan looked down at his baggy T-shirt and tracksuit bottoms. Loose fitting was the only way to cover his oversized belly and flabby muscles. At the gym near work, he hadn't looked out of place but at Perfect Bodies he didn't fit in.

Gingerly he pressed the 'start' icon on the treadmill's touchscreen control panel. It gave a judder before the belt started moving - that vibration wasn't right. Alan began a slow walk. He kept the speed steady for two minutes. Everything felt comfortable and there was no more juddering. But to do things properly he had to up the pace. He jabbed at the speed icon and the belt responded with a series of noisy judders as it rotated more quickly. Something was definitely wrong with the machine. The Usain double-turned to look.

Alan tried to appear nonchalant, as though

everything was normal but he'd pressed on the speed icon for too long and the belt was moving faster than he'd ever run before. His legs were doing their best but his breath was coming in gasps. Now the woman to his left was glancing his way as well.

"Are you OK?" she called.

Speaking was difficult so he gave her a thumbs up sign. He tried to jab at the screen again to reduce the speed but the belt had carried him backwards and he could no longer reach the control panel. He needed to go faster than the machine in order to touch the screen. With an almighty effort he powered through his legs whilst reaching forward with his upper body and stretching with his arms. The screen came tantalisingly close and he brushed it with his fingertips. But he wasn't close enough to touch the icons in a controlled manner and instead of reducing the speed it went up two notches under his flailing arms. The panel was inching from his reach again. He was perilously close to toppling off the back of the treadmill.

Through all this the machine was still juddering noisily, causing him to wobble as each foot hit the belt and his muscles had to work twice as hard to keep him upright. He was trapped in a nightmarish race against a machine.

The crash to the floor was inevitable. As he went down, he banged his chin on the edge of the treadmill platform and felt the agony of his teeth biting the soft tissue of his lips and tongue. He was vaguely aware of the Usain Bolt lookalike pressing the big red panic button on the wall and two personal trainers rushing over with a first aid box and defibrillator. After a brief argument they decided the latter wasn't necessary.

Now Suzanne was at his side helping him sit up.

"That noisy juddering is much worse at high speed, isn't it?" she said, seeming to care more about the machine than him. "At low speed it's an intermittent problem. Sometimes it happens and sometimes it doesn't. A lot of members have complained about it."

Alan nodded, not trusting himself to speak with the taste of blood in his mouth.

"That's why we called your company out again," Suzanne continued. "The engineer who came last week couldn't reproduce the problem – but he didn't get the speed up as fast as you did. You're being much more thorough. Do you think you'll be able to fix it after a rest and a coffee?"

Alan felt gingerly around his jaw and decided nothing was broken. His company kit bag, full of tools, was waiting by the treadmill. If the engineering manual for this model was in there, he might be able to repair the machine.

"I'll have a go," he said, glancing at Usain's body double who was now simultaneously sprinting and talking calmly into his mobile. Then Alan had an idea. He grinned at the perfect athlete holding the phone. "If someone else will do the testing when I've finished."

Hit or Miss?

Hit!

This story was published in *The Weekly News* in 2017.

THE PERSONAL SHOPPER

Frazer's department store was heaving with Christmas shoppers. Sonia longed to go for a coffee and take the weight off her feet but she had to get Dave something to wear to his office party that night.

"Please, Sonia," he'd said at breakfast. "I've no time to go shopping but you've got the day off. Nip into town and get me something."

"It's the day before Christmas Eve - it will be hell out there!"

"Please! It's my first Christmas party as branch manager and I don't want to let the side down. You're so good at style and I've no idea what to get for a 'do' like this."

"OK. OK. I'll go."

As she flicked crossly through the racks of clothes, Sonia wished she'd married a man who actually liked shopping. It was always the same with Dave - he reckoned he never had enough time to buy a shirt, jeans or even a pair of socks. *And* he always moaned about whatever she chose for him.

"Does this 'SALE' label mean these trousers are last year's fashion? I don't want to look stupid in the office."

"The buttons on this shirt are too fiddly to do up."

"I can't wear a pink shirt. Nobody else wears pink shirts to work."

But he never bothered to take any of it back.

As Sonia trailed past carolling reindeer and overexcited children, she decided this was the last time *ever* that she shopped for Dave's clothes. She knew exactly how she was going to dress him tonight and he wouldn't like it.

Shoes were going to be the difficult thing to buy for her husband's outfit. Dave had large, wide feet but Sonia didn't want to spend a fortune in one of the specialist shops. Money was short this Christmas and she didn't want to waste it on shoes her husband would only wear once. Eventually she found a cheap black patent pair which looked posh enough for an evening function at the Hilton. She hoped Dave would be able to dance in them without slipping over. Once he'd had a few pints, he was quite a disco animal.

His top half was next and she thanked her lucky stars when she spotted a stylish shirt with a generous cut. Knowing Dave, he'd probably quibble about the colour, so Sonia asked a sales person to check the stock room to see if they had the garment in a more subtle shade.

"Sorry, everything in that style is already on the racks," the assistant said, "but it's nice to look bright at a Christmas party, don't you think?"

HIT OR MISS?

Sonia knew Dave wouldn't agree. But she held the silky shirt against the assistant and tried to judge how it might look on Dave. It wouldn't be his first choice but, on this occasion, she reckoned he might get away with it.

When she got home, she wrote a large label, attached it to a hatpin and placed it on the pile of new clothes on the bed. Without the label he and his fellow party-goers wouldn't understand the outfit.

"Did you get my stuff?" Dave called as he arrived home from work and dropped his briefcase in the hall.

"It's in the bedroom. Try them on. And don't complain if I've bought the wrong thing. My feet are killing me after all that shopping."

"You're a star!" Dave caught Sonia beneath the mistletoe in the kitchen doorway. "I'm sorry you're not invited to the party but it was a majority office decision - no partners allowed."

Sonia didn't mind - she had no wish to be seen out with her husband in his new outfit. She was also glad that he was kissing her now, dressed in his office shirt and tie. It wouldn't seem right once he was all done up in his new clothes.

When Dave hadn't emerged from the bedroom after twenty minutes Sonia tried the door. It wouldn't open. He'd slid the bolt across.

"Can I come in?" she called.

"No, I look ridiculous," he shouted back. "And nobody will understand it."

"Don't you even like the shoes? They were a terrific bargain."

"They're too tight - even without socks on."

"Socks! You can't wear socks with that outfit. Let

me in and I'll give you a hand."

Sonia struggled to keep a straight face when she saw her husband. She reached for her mobile; this had to be recorded for posterity. Facebook was calling!

"No you don't!" Dave dived under the duvet.

"Dave, as you said, it's your first party as branch manager. You have to make the effort. Get up and I'll help you."

Reluctantly he stood before her. Sonia was enjoying herself now - all that tedious shopping had been worthwhile to see him squirm like this. She put plasters on his feet where the shoes rubbed. The green silk blouse went surprisingly well with what was left of his receding red hair. She'd wanted to get him a wig to wear for the evening - he'd look better with a full head of hair - but they were too expensive. Instead, she'd found a jaunty hat.

Then Sonia stared at her husband's odd-looking chest. The green silk bulged in a way that was definitely not natural. There hadn't been much choice on the underwear counter in his chest size and she'd had to take what she could. Sonia unfastened the tiny pearly buttons on the shirt and then felt his breasts through the bra.

"You've got one stuffed with cotton wool and one with newspaper. That's never going to look anywhere near natural!"

She emptied out the bra cups and re-stuffed both with cotton wool so that they matched.

"I bought you a pair of extra-large opaque silver tights. They'll add a touch of festive glitter. And it means you won't have to bother shaving your legs."

"Thank goodness for small mercies."

Sonia stood back and admired her handiwork.

Spotting that skirt patterned with bright red musical notes in the charity shop had been a stroke of luck. A bulge of fat sat above Dave's waistband but he'd be OK if he breathed in all night and didn't eat too much.

"Take a safety pin - just in case the button doesn't hold," she said. Then she picked up the red veiled hat that she'd found in a SALE box and placed it on his head. "Pass me the hat pin with the label. Without that no one will know who you're supposed to be."

"Why didn't you just buy me a Santa outfit or some plastic reindeer antlers? Who's going to understand this costume? I'll be embarrassed if people spend all night asking me who I am."

"Which is why we have this large name label." Sonia pushed the pin into the hat and stepped back to admire her handiwork. "Perfect, my Christmas shopping was absolutely perfect. You look like a woman, well maybe a pantomime dame, and you've got musical notes all over your skirt. It's obvious that you're going to the fancy dress party as a 'Christmas Carol'."

"I disagree." Dave was shaking his head. "It's not obvious at all. From January 1st, I resolve to buy all my own clothes - I can't risk this humiliation again."

"Result!" shouted Sonia and punched the air.

Hit or Miss

Hit!

This story was published in *The Weekly News* in 2015. It was inspired by all the men who sit back and let their wives do their clothes shopping. I wonder if the pandemic boom in online shopping has changed things?

THE CHECKLIST

Like most women, Wendy had a checklist of what constituted the perfect male. It had been finely honed since she got divorced and started dating again. She'd even trained her daughter in its usefulness. Wendy mentally referred to the list whenever a new man came along, especially during those early days of first impressions and getting-to-know-you conversations. She had no hesitation in using it when she was first introduced to Simon.

They met over dinner in Wendy's favourite Italian restaurant. The lighting was subdued and there were candles on the tables. Simon was already examining the menu when Wendy arrived but when he saw her, he stood up, smiled and shook her hand. His good manners earned him his first tick on the list and he also got an extra credit for the way his eyes twinkled with his smile.

"It's lovely to meet you, Wendy."

"And you, Simon." She liked the way he used her name without awkwardness.

There were three of them around the table for that first meal but Simon was the only one Wendy was interested in. Their eyes kept accidentally meeting as she checked the list in her head and then glanced at him to make sure he made the grade. He used the right cutlery for his seafood starter and handled his spaghetti main course with aplomb, niftily twisting the pasta around his fork. No trail of tomato sauce dripped down his shirt.

"What do you do for a living, Wendy?" He paused, fork in hand, and looked directly at her.

"I'm a mechanical engineer."

Men were usually stunned into silence when she mentioned her job but Simon wasn't fazed. He wanted to know specifically what the job entailed. It was refreshing to find a man interested in a woman's career and mentally she ticked several checklist boxes. Wendy's ex-husband had always resented the fact that she earned more than him and he'd tried to persuade their daughter, Chloe, to take a clerical job instead of becoming an accountant. That had incensed Wendy. His lack of encouragement and ambition for their daughter was one of the things that had driven them apart. Despite her father's disparaging remarks, Chloe had qualified as a chartered accountant and now worked for one of the top city firms. Wendy was proud and hoped her daughter would eventually find a partner who'd be willing to give Chloe's career the same importance as their own.

After a discussion about the design of the aeroplane engines that Wendy worked on, the conversation between the three of them widened to more general topics. Simon laughed easily and the mood at their table was relaxed. When a birthday cake was brought to the adjacent table, they joined in with the singing. Wendy gladly noted that Simon was a social animal who knew how to enjoy himself without needing copious amounts of alcohol to get in the right mood.

As they parted outside the restaurant Simon had to stoop in order to kiss her on the cheek. This was another tick on the list. It probably seemed old fashioned, especially given her macho work environment, but Wendy liked a tall man. Overall, Simon seemed confident without being cocky but Wendy felt the need to see him again before she could consider her checklist complete and be absolutely sure that he was Mr Right and worth investing in emotionally, for both her and Chloe's sakes.

"What did you think, Mum?" Chloe was familiar with her mother's checklist and was on the phone first thing the next morning to find out whether or not Simon had made the grade. "Did he pass the test?"

"He's definitely over the first hurdle. First impressions were good but I want to see him again. It would be nice to invite him here for Sunday lunch - it seems the right thing to do since he paid last night. But, as you know my cooking's not brilliant, what if he's got a checklist on me? I don't want to upset the applecart with someone this promising!"

"Men aren't like that, Mum. And especially not in this case, I'm sure about that. But I could make you a starter and a pudding. I'll drop them off early so Simon won't find out. All you'll have to do is buy one of those ready-to-roast joints, some frozen Yorkshire puddings and some vegetables."

"Will he be able to tell it's not all homemade?" Because Simon had ticked so many boxes Wendy was nervous. He was well on his way to being that elusive Mr Right and she didn't want to put him off with her poor culinary skills.

"He's just an ordinary man, Mum, not a MasterChef judge."

Wendy spent Saturday dusting, vacuuming and polishing. By inviting Simon to her home, she'd inadvertently turned the tables and put herself up for scrutiny. But at least it would give her chance to go through the remaining important points on her mental list - those that could only be checked in a domestic setting.

"These are for you, Wendy." Simon handed her a large bouquet of carnations and gypsophila as he arrived.

She mentally ticked 'Suitable gift for the hostess' on her checklist.

"Greek salad - my favourite," said Chloe diplomatically, as Wendy served the starters. As promised, her daughter didn't mention that the salad was her own creation.

It was surprisingly good and the chocolate mousse that Chloe had provided for pudding was delicious too. Chloe had always been a better cook than Wendy but, judging by these two examples, her daughter's culinary skills were getting even better.

Simon helped clear away and wash up. This was the final bit that Wendy had invited him here to check on - his domesticity. A career woman needs an equal partner, someone who will shoulder his share of the domestic chores. Wendy's ex-husband had failed miserably in that area. When Chloe was young Wendy had been in a constant state of exhaustion trying to work full-time, be a mum and also shouldering nearly all the housework as well. She wasn't going to let history repeat itself.

"Where does this go?" Simon asked, indicating Chloe's salad dish, just as Wendy's daughter walked into the kitchen.

Wendy hesitated. In order to keep up the charade that she had cooked the whole meal, she needed to put the salad bowl away in her own cupboard. But Chloe was looking at her in a strange way, as though she was about to speak. Then her daughter went and stood next to her boyfriend.

"We'd better come clean." Chloe slipped her arm around Simon's waist. "It's confession time, Mum. I didn't make the salad or the mousse. Simon made them both."

"What?" Wendy was confused and embarrassed. Then she realised this revelation deserved a huge gold star on her daughter's boyfriend's checklist - a man who is willing to cook is beyond price. Her smile told Chloe that Simon had passed all the tests and that the couple had Wendy's blessing. Simon was going to be a perfectly suitable son-in-law. Wendy just hoped she'd passed muster with him as a prospective mother-in-law.

THE CHECKLIST

<u>Hit or Miss?</u>

Miss.

'The Checklist' was rejected by *My Weekly* and *The Weekly News*. In fact, it was rejected twice by the latter publication because I tried it with two different fiction editors. The idea was triggered by the judgements, conscious or unconscious, we all make when our offspring bring home a new partner for the first time.

THE SAME BUT DIFFERENT

What was it the first man on the moon said? Something like, "One small step for man but one huge leap for mankind"? Today I feel like that astronaut.

"Come on, Kathleen," Jim's saying, "put your coat on and let's get this over with. You know it's for the best."

I remain rooted to the spot in the kitchen. I can hear our son, David, moving around in his bedroom overhead. The thudding of his music is comforting. It means that all is well in his world – which makes everything alright in my world too. But David doesn't know that very soon I'm going to turn his world upside down.

"Kathleen! We didn't do all that decorating for nothing." Jim hands me my coat and goes to call David.

Decorating the new place was the easy bit – once

we'd found the right wallpaper. The stuff we needed had been discontinued years ago. The last time we bought that pattern it was in a remnant sale and we only just managed to cobble together enough rolls then from the same batch. This time we trailed round DIY stores, scoured the internet and paged through endless pattern books looking for paper that was light beige with flecks of just the right shade of brown. Finally, David spotted it in a book which I'd already been through and discounted. But if he thought it was acceptable then I was happy with it too. David was the one who'd have to live with it.

"It's the same but different," he'd said, running his fingers over the textured page.

"David!" Jim is shouting up the stairs now.

"He can't hear you with the door shut and his music on. You'll have to go and knock."

Jim huffs, puffs and generally makes a fuss about having to walk up the stairs to remind our adult son that it's time to leave. Usually it's me that takes charge, gets things done and sends the family off to wherever they should be – work, hospital appointment or college, but today I can't. I just can't.

I can't eat breakfast, I can't do my face and I can't manage more than a sip of my tea. It's gone stone cold whilst I've been standing here looking at it. I can barely put my arms in my coat sleeves and fasten the buttons.

"David, have you forgotten?" Jim is talking loudly over the music which is bouncing decibels down the stairs now the bedroom door has been opened. "We said we'd leave at 11 o'clock – it's nearly 10 past now."

I visualise Jim tapping his watch in David's face

and David shaking his head blankly – time is an alien concept to him. Left to his own devices, life would consist of loud music, late night computer games and too much takeaway food delivered to the door.

Getting ready for today has cost a lot of money – making the new place "the same but different" has meant we couldn't just go for a bargain. It's been a struggle to find the cash especially since Jim's overtime's been cut. I haven't worked since David was born. He wasn't the sort of baby that would be welcome in a nursery, besides I'd brought him into the world and felt responsible for him. I loved him too. Not immediately, but when I'd got used to him and especially when he started to smile at seven months old. That's when we discovered he was ticklish and he still is. I can't resist tracing my finger lightly over his bare feet when he's got them up on the settee.

"He's ready, Kathleen. Let's go."

Somehow I run a comb through my hair and find my bag.

"Have you got the key to the room?" Jim asks. "I don't want to get there and find we can't get in."

Hope lurches in my heart. If the key is lost then we can stay as we are. No-one will have to go anywhere. Someone else can have that same but different room – someone who needs it much more than us, someone whose family are at the desperate end-of-their-tether stage.

Jim won't let us get into that terrible state. He worries too much about the future and what might happen. Jim has to have a plan. That's what started this whole moving business off. Six months ago Jim brought up the death question yet again.

"If anything happens to you, Kathleen," he said. "I can't manage on my own."

I knew he was right. It wasn't just the cooking and housework - it's the more intimate stuff that Jim can't stomach. Maybe it's because I'm a woman that I can manage the caring side better.

"And if anything happens to me," he went on. "I don't want you to be trapped here in an ever-shrinking world."

To me a shrinking world didn't matter if David was happy. But if that mysterious "something" did happen to Jim and then I got ill or fainted or even collapsed and died, it could be days before anyone discovered what had happened and then it might be too late for David. He wouldn't be able to fetch help.

So, we'd spoken to Social Services and they'd offered us the room. During the last month we'd tried to involve David to make the transition as easy as possible. As I said, the wallpaper was the hardest thing to duplicate. His desk and book case are fairly recent chain store purchases so they were easily found. The bed is conveniently non-descript and the bedding is all standard white with a *Star Wars* duvet cover which is still in production. I bought three identical duvet covers to allow for washing and accidents. David can't handle change; everything has to be familiar.

Jim unearths the key for the new room from the hall table and I swallow hard.

"Don't forget your laptop," I say to David automatically – he takes that machine everywhere. In some ways it's a godsend and others a curse.

The car feels stuffy and airless. I want to grab the wheel from Jim and turn us around. This isn't how families are supposed to act. They don't expel one member and make him go and live somewhere else. We're not wild animals competing for supremacy in the herd where the weakest will be left to die. Other people think I should be happy that David's leaving home.

"It'll be a weight off your shoulders when he's gone," one said. "At last you'll have some 'me' time."

I'm not sure what 'me' time is. I have plenty of opportunity to knit and watch TV now, with David here on his laptop or plugged into his music. After today there'll be a huge hole that no end of wool or soap operas will fill.

"When our Susie went off to work in London we saved no end of money," another friend told me. "She was always in the shower, on the phone or bringing friends round to eat. As soon as she went our bills plummeted."

I thought this person might have realised that not only was David not a typical twenty-year-old girl but also, unlike Susie, he hadn't chosen to leave. We, his parents, have taken the decision to kick him out of the only home he's ever known, like he's some impossible to live with monster.

"Can you remember where we're going today, David?" Jim asks, as we get through the one-way system.

"Shopping!"

There's a note of triumph in his voice because he thinks he's right. I start to cry. Jim throws me a warning look – if David sees me upset then he'll start wailing too. I bury my wet face in my handbag, looking for a tissue.

As soon as we pull up outside the low-rise

building the warden rushes out to greet us. She's my age and reassuringly plump. She speaks directly to my son.

"Hello, David."

He looks blankly at her and then turns to us, puzzled.

"Let's go and see your room," I suggest brightly, forcing a smile and propelling him forward. "You can be in charge."

I hand him the key and he fumbles with the lock. When he succeeds in opening the door, he grins like he's won the lottery. A tight feeling begins in my throat and travels to my heart.

David sits on the familiar duvet cover and smiles at the same posters he's got at home. He stands up and fingers them. As far as possible I positioned the technicolour footballers exactly as they are in his room at home.

"The same but different," my son proclaims.

"It's only for a few nights," I gabble not knowing if he's realised he's going to be staying here without us. "You can come home at weekends and phone us whenever you want."

He ignores me and starts setting up his laptop next to a small stereo, identical to the one he had for Christmas. I bury my head in my handbag again.

When I look up, David is staring down at me. I recognise the contorted anguish on his face – it means he's recognised my mood and is going to cry too.

"Let's get this machine booted up," Jim says with over-enthusiastic cheeriness.

The computer games are our standard distraction technique – but this time David doesn't bite. He emits a small wail. Maternal instinct propels me towards him.

"High five!"

I jump at the interruption and we all turn towards the new, deep, male voice.

"High five!" The newcomer, a young man, repeats and advances on David, his hand raised.

"High five!" mimics my son and their palms meet in a slap.

"This is Timothy," explains the warden. "His room is next door."

David's face is relaxed now and he's busy with the laptop mouse whilst Timothy watches over his shoulder. A seed of hope drops into the gloomy mud of my mind — friendships have been few and far between for my son. This looks like a new beginning.

The warden gestures for us to leave whilst the going is good. I want to kiss David goodbye, stroke his hair and breathe in his scent. But the warden is gently pushing us out of the room.

"Mum and Dad are going, David," she says. "Why don't you show Timothy how to play your favourite game?"

She shuts the door behind us and Jim and I stand in the corridor staring at the closed door. Neither of us makes a move to leave. I want to howl like a lioness deprived of her cub. Jim is blinking hard.

"They said to leave it a few days before visiting," my husband says in a strange voice. "Give him time to settle."

I nod, wondering how I'll bear it and what we'll do to fill the gap. I can't remember the last time Jim and I were on our own together. But more importantly, how will David bear it?

There's a sort of squeal from behind the door. Immediately I grab the knob, ready to push it open and rescue my son.

Jim puts his hand on mine. "No, Kathleen. We have to be cruel to be kind."

My heart wants to break through the door and envelop my cub. But my mind recognises the truth uttered by Jim. Through willpower, I stop myself giving in to maternal instinct.

Jim presses his ear to the door. I don't want him to tell me about the anguish he can hear within. But he smiles and motions me to copy him. Reluctantly I lean the side of my head against the door.

There are more squealing noises but there's something else too. It sounds like laughter, David's laughter mixed with that of another boy. Something that's been so rare in the past two decades. My son is enjoying himself with a new friend.

"I think it's going to be alright," I say. "Let's go home."

Jim returns my grin.

Hit or Miss?

Hit!

This story was published in *The People's Friend* in 2019 under the title, 'Time to Fly'.

LOOKALIKE

It was Philippa's first audition to be a professional lookalike and it felt weird. More than weird. It was like being in a fairground hall of mirrors, surrounded by distorted images of herself. She was surrounded by Philippas in every combination of shape and size. Now she knew how she would have looked, had genes made her taller, smaller, fatter or thinner.

"Where do you think she's disappeared to?" The girl in front of Philippa in the queue had turned around to talk.

"Who?"

"Fee-Fee Malone, of course. She's the reason we're all queuing up like slightly gone-wrong clones of her and each other. I'd love to be her in real life instead of just her paid lookalike. Think of all that money!"

"Who knows where she is? Probably living the high life in Brazil or some other place that has no extradition treaty." Philippa had read all the news stories about Fee-Fee Malone. Pop singer, Steve Stardust, had fallen madly in love with Fee-Fee and then she'd done a runner, taking much of his fortune with her.

"Imagine being clever enough to con a rock star out of his wealth like that," the other girl continued. "They say she used to be something in the city and knew about money and legal stuff. She tricked him into putting his cash into her name. I'm Chelsea, by the way."

"Philippa." Philippa didn't want to speculate about Fee-Fee but she couldn't turn away from Chelsea without seeming rude. Philippa had been something in the city once. It had been long hours and continuous, stressful rounds of redundancies. When her name had finally appeared on the list of those to be terminated, relief had been her overriding emotion – until the severance package was revealed as only the statutory state minimum and she was forced to flee London's high rents. But every cloud has a silver lining. Philippa had made the situation work for her and now she was back living in the capital.

"Have you been a lookalike before?" Chelsea changed the subject.

"No. Until Fee-Fee I've never looked like a famous person."

"I bought a long black wig and auditioned as Cher once but they said my eyebrows let me down. I should've dyed them. Take my advice - being a lookalike is all about getting the small details right."

Philippa nodded and turned to scan the rest of the room. Fee-Fee was a natural blonde, like her and Chelsea, but it was obvious that a lot of the wannabes here had used colour from a bottle that wasn't quite the right shade. Philippa didn't rate their chances of getting through the audition, not with Steve Stardust himself on the judging panel. The sudden thought of Steve's scrutiny in just a few minutes made Philippa's heart thump with nerves.

"My boyfriend is in the next room," Chelsea said. "He's trying out for Lord Lucan. Apparently, they're scouring stables for a Shergar lookalike too. Good idea, isn't it, to make a TV program about famous disappearances?"

"I guess." Philippa thought all the publicity around Fee-Fee was a bad idea. Fee-Fee's rise to fame as Steve Stardust's girlfriend and then her disappearance with his fortune meant people were stopping Philippa in the street and asking what she'd done with the money. Even when she said she wasn't Fee-Fee some of them still tried to grab her in a selfie or follow her down the street. To turn things to her advantage and to stop people accusing her of being the real thing, Philippa had decided to become a bona fide fee-earning lookalike, even though she didn't need the money.

"Steve Stardust deserved what he got," Philippa said to Chelsea. "The papers said he voluntarily signed the money over to her to avoid the tax. If he'd been honest about paying his dues he'd still be sitting on his fortune."

Then suddenly they were at the front of the queue. A three-strong selection panel sat immediately before the stage. Chelsea went first. Her face brightened as though a switch had been pulled and she paraded in front of the panel with a swagger and a toothy grin that Philippa thought was nothing like Fee-Fee

Malone. One of the selectors turned towards Philippa's side of the stage. His face was momentarily caught in the spotlight that had tracked Chelsea across the stage. Steve Stardust. Philippa recognised him even in his dark glasses and sober suit. She'd known he'd be here but still she felt nervous. Her palms went damp. Now she had the impossible task of appearing exactly like Fee-Fee Malone but also essentially different. The usher was pushing her forward ready for her turn to walk across the stage. She felt sick but the spotlight had caught her and now there was no turning back. She paraded. Remembering Chelsea's swagger, she concentrated on how she walked – exactly the same as Fee-Fee but essentially different.

"That one again, please," Steve said.

The usher on the opposite side of the stage turned her around. Philippa was trembling. To win this part in the TV program would be perfect. She would officially be a lookalike of Fee-Fee Malone. Then, when interest in the scandal had died down, she could go back to a quiet life. But Philippa couldn't risk being too perfect a clone and Steve's presence here was making that almost impossible. She walked back onto the stage and the casting director, the middle member of the panel, signalled her to stop in front of them. Her cheeks began to burn under Steve's gaze and her knees felt weak.

"She's painted the birthmark on her neck perfectly. The similarity to Fee-Fee is brilliant." Steve took off his dark glasses and beckoned her closer. "If I didn't know that Fee-Fee herself wouldn't have the brazen cheek to show up here…"

Trembling Philippa took a very small step forward.

Steve motioned with his hand again and she had no option but to move closer, glad she'd taken the precautionary measure of changing from her usual distinctive perfume. His eyes ran over her body from head to toe, lingering on her face. He made a circular motion with his hand and she slowly turned around. Her heart was racing and her mouth was dry. Fabricated explanations and excuses raced through her head. None of them would be believed if she was questioned.

"Feebs – we're going to be the dream team."

Her mind jumped but she managed to maintain her outward composure. It was the phrase Steve had used so often when they were together. As his girlfriend she'd always whispered back, 'Together we create real stardust.' But now she said, "Absolutely, Steve," and raised her hand to high-five him – a gesture Steve would recognise as completely abhorrent to the real Fee-Fee.

Steve gave a nod to the casting director, who ticked a list in front of him and said, "You're through to the next round. Wait over there."

Philippa found a seat at the other side of the hall. Relief sagged her shoulders. That had been a close call. Hiding in plain sight as a professional lookalike for herself, Fee-Fee Malone, was a gamble but, if she could pull it off, it was far better than fleeing to Brazil.

Hit or Miss?

Hit!

Lookalike was published in *The Weekly News* in 2019.

FEAR OF FLYING

"We have now reached our cruising altitude. I wish you an enjoyable flight." There was a click as the cockpit intercom was switched off.

"He sounds young, doesn't he?" The lady sitting in the aisle seat next to Fiona loosened her seatbelt.

"Yes." Anxiety made Fiona monosyllabic.

"The landing in Funchal is one of the most difficult in the world," the lady continued. "The pilots have to go on a special training course."

"I know." Fiona took deep breaths, trying not to let her anxiety get out of proportion.

"You're not scared of flying, are you? You look awfully pale."

Fiona tried to smile. "Six am take-offs don't suit me. I'll be fine once I've had coffee."

"I'm Marjorie by the way."

"Fiona."

Fiona closed her eyes. An image of her son Joe

appeared. It was at Palma airport twenty years ago as they waited for the flight home. He was racing round the departure lounge with a model plane in each hand making jet engine noises. He'd spent the whole fortnight of their holiday counting the sleeps until they could get back on the plane and fly home. He loved soaring into the sky. Fiona was the opposite. She was only making this flight for Joe's sake.

"Coffee's here!" Marjorie's elbow nudged her and the stewardess handed over paper cups.

"What's the wind like over Funchal?" Marjorie asked.

The stewardess hesitated. "Strong but air traffic control is hopeful it will subside shortly."

Marjorie sat back in her seat with a satisfied smile. "Two years ago it was too windy and we had three aborted landings. Down we went. The wheels were almost on the runway and then we accelerated upwards again." Her arm illustrated a steep descent followed by an almost vertical ascent. "The poor girl next to me was sick and her mother was crying."

"I don't want to know."

"Then we had to divert to Faro before we ran out of fuel. We got a night in a five star hotel. It was very exciting!"

Trapped in the middle seat Fiona sipped her coffee and tried to discourage further gruesome tales from her neighbour by looking the other way. The man in the window seat swiftly changed the angle of his newspaper so she couldn't read over his shoulder.

Fiona had checked the weather forecast last night and again on her phone in the departure lounge this morning.

"Don't fuss, Mum," Joe had said. "Air traffic

control won't let planes land if it's too windy."

She was flying for a week in the sunshine with her son, daughter-in-law and grandchildren. It had been a last-minute decision once Joe's work rota came out, consequently their seats were spread across the cabin. After some negotiation with the crew, her daughter-in-law at least had been able to sit with her twin three-year-olds. They were up by the cockpit and there was no sound of tantrums so Fiona assumed everything was OK.

The intercom clicked on again and the captain gave an update on the route they were taking. Then he warned them about a windy approach into Funchal.

"Such a young sounding person with all these lives in his hands," Marjorie said and then opened a thick paperback book.

Fiona managed to doze until she heard a faint ping and the seatbelt lights came on for landing.

"Don't worry, the little ones are fine." The stewardess who'd sorted out the seats for the twins patted Fiona on the shoulder as she went down the cabin checking seatbelts. "And Joe's doing good too."

Now they were on the final approach. Marjorie offered Fiona a boiled sweet and she concentrated on the artificial sweetness on her tongue rather than the growing closeness of land.

Just as she was braced for wheels on tarmac the plane accelerated upwards. Fiona gripped the arms of her seat. All she could think about was Joe and what must be going through his mind. At heart he was still the little boy with the model planes. She wanted to rush up there and help him through this, just as she'd taught him to ride a bike and drive a car.

A second landing attempt was announced on the intercom. Fiona refused another boiled sweet and sent all her mental energy to her son. It wasn't enough. Again there was acceleration and a steep ascent.

The next update from the cockpit announced that, due to fuel levels, this would be their final landing attempt. Fiona felt the old lady touch her hand. She held it tightly.

The wheels went down and hit the tarmac. There was a huge cheer from the passengers and Fiona thought her heart would burst with pride.

"He did it!" she said to Marjorie. "My son just captained his first flight into Funchal!"

Hit or Miss?

Hit!

'Fear of Flying' won the monthly 'flash' competition in *Writers' Forum* in September 2018. The brief for this particular competition was to write a 'risky' story for the women's magazine fiction market. The inspiration came from my own experience of a holiday flight into Funchal which failed to land three times because of high winds and had to divert to Faro.

CAREER CHANGE

Chardonnay was determined not to be a barista forever. The pace of work was relentless, the queue of customers endless and the repetition of coffee making monotonous. She was fed up of the rich smell of roasted coffee beans and no longer wanted the free, unsold cakes offered to staff at the end of the day. However, there was one positive - two doors down from the Haven Artisan Café, on Tottenham Court Road, was Maxim's Model Agency. Maxim looked like Mr Toad, he always drummed his fingers impatiently in the queue and was quick to complain if his coffee wasn't made exactly as he liked it. But Chardonnay could forgive all this because she wanted to impress him. He would be the key to her escape to a better life. Maxim could help Chardonnay achieve her ambition of becoming a model - if only she could make him notice her potential.

She hatched a plan and manipulated the staff rota

to put herself on shift whenever the amphibian called in for his caffeine fix. His routine never varied: an early morning three-shot cappuccino to-go on Monday, a leisurely latte on Friday afternoon and a Wednesday lunchtime business meeting. Chardonnay's supervisor, Orlando, didn't like these meetings, he thought they tied up his tables for too long without sufficient profit but Chardonnay loved them. They gave her an excuse to saunter past Maxim and his colleagues in the manner of a tall, willowy catwalk model. She asked them if everything was alright, with a flash of her whitened teeth and a flick of her straightened, long blonde hair - a gesture guaranteed to please the most fastidious fashion editor or the fussiest photographer. Surely Maxim would realise she was perfect for shampoo or toothpaste adverts or even a Vogue photo-shoot. Orlando got cross whenever he noticed she'd let down her hair. He would quote Health and Safety rules and Chardonnay had to hurriedly gather up her pony tail and sit the silly yellow company baseball cap back on top.

"Stop fawning over Maxim and his cronies," Orlando said to her one day. "There are other customers to serve and other tables to clear. If you want to be a model, send in a portfolio like everyone else."

But Chardonnay couldn't afford a professional portfolio of pictures. Her only chance was to impress Maxim while she had him as a captive audience. Noticing Maxim's chair was facing the counter and that he occasionally glanced across, she concentrated on her posture as she clipped the corners off plastic milk bags, sprinkled cocoa powder on cappuccinos, reached for flavoured syrups from the shelf and pulled the levers of the big, silver coffee beast. Stomach muscles in. Shoulders back. Think tall. Smile in case he's looking this way. Chardonnay was going to make sure that one day this minimum wage servitude would be a distant memory. One day the glamourous world of the catwalk and camera would be her reality. Riches and red carpets awaited her. Chardonnay was made for something better.

"I could create a portfolio for you to give to Maxim," Orlando suggested one day. "I'm sick of the way your starry eyes mean you don't see customers and sticky tables. The only thing you clean properly is the coffee machine because you can see your reflection in it. Once you're gone, I can get a proper assistant with short hair and an interest in customer service."

Chardonnay was tempted by Orlando's offer. But she'd seen his holiday selfies and they weren't even fit for Facebook.

"I've got a proper camera," he continued as if reading her mind, "with different lenses and a white balance setting and stuff. It was a bargain on EBay."

"OK. But I only hand over the photos to Maxim if they're any good." She wasn't going to let Orlando ruin her prospects, whatever he thought about her attitude in the café.

They did the shoot in Regent's Park on a sunny day. Orlando talked incomprehensibly about light and shade. Passers-by stared and Chardonnay strutted her stuff, feeling like a real model. Orlando laughed when she started waving imperially, like the Queen. She hadn't meant to, it just happened and his laughter made her feel small. She tried to hide her humiliation by consulting the list she'd made on her phone. It contained all the necessary poses: full length, seated, head and shoulder and even pictures of her hands – in case a nail polish advert came up.

The quality of the finished photographs surprised Chardonnay and she planted a kiss of gratitude on Orlando's cheek. He blushed and touched the side of his face with his hand.

Maxim was surprised to be handed a large brown envelope with his next cappuccino but he promised to take a look. He called Chardonnay's mobile when she was wiping tables later that morning.

"Loved the pictures," he said.

She almost dropped the phone.

"You're a natural for our next shoot," he went on. "Catalogue shopping is coming back and we've just landed a big contract."

In her imagination the cameras were clicking, directors were asking her to turn this way and that, makeup girls were touching up her lips and eyes, a stylist was admiring the way the clothes hung and swung on her size eight figure. Catwalk agents were watching from the wings and …

"Chardonnay! There's a rush. I need you!"

Orlando's words skimmed over her head leaving no imprint. Her eyes didn't see the lengthening queue of people at the counter. Instead of thirsty riff-raff she saw designer outfits in a brightly lit studio, instead of day-old sandwiches she saw Champagne and canapes for between shot nibbles.

Chardonnay took her P45 and said goodbye to Orlando and the poverty prison of the Haven Artisan Café and hello to the moneyed freedom of the freelance photographic model.

CAREER CHANGE

***

Chardonnay was determined not to be a catalogue model forever. The pace of work was relentless, the queue of garments endless and the repetition of pose holding monotonous. She sweated under the heat from the lights and the muscles in her face ached from a continuous smile. However, there was one positive – she'd met a girl whose boyfriend supervised cabin crew for a major airline. He would be her key to escaping to a better life travelling the globe. She hatched a plan and she and the girl now shared a flat. Chardonnay made sure she was always around when the girl's boyfriend called. She showcased her talents by serving him a selection of drinks and snacks and speaking with gestures that showed her natural talent for demonstrating lifejackets and emergency exits.

All day in the studio she posed in jeans, jackets and jumpers with her long hair cascading over her shoulders. But in her head, she wore court shoes and a pencil skirt with her hair in a bun beneath a natty little hat.

Soon she'd escape the fenced-in, flashbulb world of fashion and fly free to all four corners of the world.

She sent Orlando a text about her plans for another career move. He responded immediately, "Aren't cabin crew baristas by another name?"

Hit or Miss?

Hit!

'Career Change' was published in *The Weekly News* in 2017. It was originally written for a competition with the theme 'the grass is always greener'.

LOCAL FLASH FICTION

The three very short stories below were entered into FOLIO Sutton Coldfield flash fiction competitions in 2020 and 2021. Two of them were placed and one was not. Can you rank the stories in the correct order?

Rules: A maximum of 250 words per story and the subject matter must have a connection to Sutton Coldfield, a town to the north of Birmingham in England.

I Kissed Paul McCartney

"I kissed Paul McCartney."

Chantelle pauses, mid-pierce, over the plastic lasagne. For a moment she thinks I've said something interesting. Then she remembers her client is a seventy-one-year-old dementia victim and plunges the fork in again.

"They played Sutton Coldfield just once. February 1963, Maney Hall." I talk quickly, Chantelle has only twenty minutes. "I was fourteen and he was …" The artificial food twirls in the microwave. Chantelle strokes her phone. The word is simultaneously on the tip of my tongue and in the unreachable basement of my mind. "… not ugly." The words aren't right but the meaning's there.

Chantelle shoves her phone into her overall pocket.

"Their first song wasn't great." The song title floats where I can't reach it. "My friend Sheila was happy to drink orange juice and wait to be asked to dance but I got a pass-out and ran to the Horse and Jockey for a vodka and lemon. Underage didn't matter then."

Chantelle's expression says she's not listening and even if she was, she wouldn't believe me.

"When I got back, the Beatles were loading their blue Commer. I held the back door of the hall for them. 'Thanks, love,' Paul said. He went to kiss my cheek but I turned my head and we kissed on the lips."

It's nearly time for Chantelle to leave.

"John Lennon told him to hurry up because they had to get to Tamworth."

"And pigs might fly." The front door bangs behind my carer.

Local connection: The Beatles really did play at Maney Hall in February 1963, followed by a second gig on the same night in the nearby town of Tamworth.

Nicholas Brown's Diary 23rd January 1955

Audrey had her disappointed look again. She directed it first at the meagre slice of bread and one egg on the plate between us. Then at me, as though I was to blame for our current situation.

"It's not my fault British Leyland is laying people off."

"Maybe not." She stroked the round of her belly. Her voice was bitter. "But fresh air doesn't feed a child."

I slunk to the Labour Exchange. The queue was long and they had nothing for me. Again. Afterwards I stayed in the park to delay taking further disappointment to Audrey. I was at Town Gate when it happened.

The noise was a gunshot, bomb and earthquake rolled into one. A soldier's instinct pushed me to the ground. The silence was louder than the noise. Screams. This time I ran towards instead of away. The station was a mangle of broken train. A woman had been thrown clear. I could hardly look at the mess of her. She whimpered like a dog. Her hand twitched. I reached for it and she clutched my finger like a baby. I thought of our bump and the future. The woman's last breath was an exchange. New life for old.

I was crying and stroking her hair when Audrey found me. She led me away.

"You did the right thing," my wife said. "No one should die alone."

Then I was in her arms and the morning's resentment was gone: disappeared into the knowledge that life is finite.

Local connection: There was a terrible train crash in Sutton Coldfield in 1955 which killed seventeen people.

Bovine Protest

The Sutton Coldfield Pensioners' Action Group grinned from their individual Zoom windows. Cedric felt as though he was starring in an old episode of *Celebrity Squares*.

"Are we ready?" he asked.

"Absolutely." His vice chair, Shirley, gave a thumbs up.

"Over to you, Nate."

The sixteen-year-old flicked his floppy fringe and attacked his smartphone. Nate had explained the technology several times but it was still smoke and mirrors to his granddad. Cedric couldn't comprehend what was happening up in the clouds and behind the virtual fences or whatever the terminology was that Nate had used. It was something to do with the cows' orange collars.

On screen Nate was looking through a curtain of hair and checking off the actions:

1. Computer controlling virtual fencing hacked.
2. Virtual fencing changed to funnel cows towards Banners Gate.
3. Banners Gate entrance unsecured.

4. Sutton Coldfield Youth Action Group in position with banners.
5. Traffic stopped.

"Now!" Excitement flashed across the teenager's face and he was replaced by a webcam view of the Monmouth Drive/Chester Road junction. Cows plodded into the road as if guided by an unseen hand. The camera panned to the teenagers with placards.

"Save our Planet – No More Beef Cattle!" "Veg not Steak!" "No More Global Warming!"

"Hooray!" Shirley sounded like an over-excited football fan, her wheelchair coming into shot as she swayed from side to side. "Even in the winter of our years we can still help ensure the next generation enjoys their spring."

Local connection: Sutton Park is a 2,400 acre National Nature Reserve and was given to the town by Henry VIII. It's one of the largest urban parks in Europe and is designated as a Site of Special Scientific Interest. Every summer cows are brought into the park for grazing and in recent years they have been fitted with GPS collars to facilitate virtual fencing. This stops the cows wandering into places they are not wanted, such as the local golf course. The animal receives an audible warning from the collar as it approaches a virtual fence line, followed by a short electric pulse if it then reaches the line.

Local Flash Fiction – Competition Ranking

'I Kissed Paul McCartney' was placed First in the 2020 competition.

'Bovine Protest' was placed Second in the 2021 competition.

'Nicholas Brown's Diary 23rd January 1955' was unplaced in the 2021 competition.

MARATHON MADNESS

Dave's running-club vest was sticking to him, his hair felt damp against his forehead and a trickle of sweat was running down his spine. He'd known the marathon was going to be tough and that he could expect to be on his feet for well over four hours - but he hadn't expected it to be this hard.

It was the mass of people that was making things difficult. He'd thought that by now, at mile fifteen, things would've thinned out. He'd expected the elite runners to be haring off at almost a sprint and the fancy dress fun runners to be dawdling with their charity collecting tins, leaving Joe Average to plod along at a steady pace and not cause him too much hassle. Instead, a constant torrent of people was pushing past.

The drinks station was manic and caused the crowd to lose the rhythm of their running – some were slowing down to swig water whilst others just wanted to sprint through without refreshment. Inevitably there were collisions and the use of choice language.

Dave wasn't sure he could stay the course anymore. He was struggling to keep up with the flow of runners in front of him. They were sticking their arms out like windmills to snatch a bottle of water whilst on the move. It was more by luck than judgement that one of their out-stretched hands didn't thump someone in the face.

Dave paused for a moment and raised his own bottle to his lips. When he looked up, ready to continue, a new group were in front of him – panting, sweating and cursing.

The heat was starting to make him feel dizzy. He clenched his fists and willed the fuzzy, faint feeling to go away – despite everything he was enjoying himself and didn't want to give up now. He sipped his water again but it made him feel no better. If anything, it was making him feel sick.

"Dave!" A tiger, in trainers and sporting a running number, gave him a slap on the back as he ran past. "Keep it up!"

Dave found it impossible to believe that anyone could run 26 miles dressed in fur on a day as hot as today. In fact, right now, 26 miles in any sort of outfit seemed an impossible distance to cover.

"You're not looking good, mate." One of the marshals had come alongside him. "Do you need to take a break? Maybe find some shade – try going under the trees on the opposite side of the road."

"I'm fine," Dave lied. "Energy reserves are a bit low but I can soon sort that."

He took an energy gel pack from his shorts'

pocket, tore it open with his teeth and squeezed it into his mouth. It was too sweet to be pleasant but ought to give him a blood sugar boost to stop him fainting before the end.

The lads at the running club had talked him into this escapade because they needed to fulfil their quota of people. "It'll be good for you," one of them had said. "It'll give you some experience of the atmosphere of a marathon so that if you get through the ballot and into the London next year, it won't all be such a shock."

He'd been too much of a wimp to admit that he had no intention of entering any marathon, and certainly not the London, in the near future. So here he was – just to make up the numbers.

"Dave!" Jim, the club's seventy-year-old veteran captain, had come alongside him. "You are just what I need." Jim snatched the water bottle from Dave's hand. "It was great that you could be here and complete our team – gives us credibility when we can field this many people."

The old man was soon lost amongst the runners further down the course and Dave found himself left with the stragglers. His legs felt heavy and awkward and his breathing had become laboured. If he concentrated hard this awful feeling might go away so that he could make it through the event. If he had to drop out the lads at the club would never let him live it down. He looked at his watch and guessed he had another half an hour on his feet before the end.

He took several deep breaths but then things went orange and blurry. The ground came up and smacked him in the face before everything went black.

Now, a St. John's Ambulance man was shaking

him and asking where his running number was.

Dave felt mortified. Hundreds of runners had completed 26 miles today, whilst he'd merely been standing behind a table, handing out bottles of water to them. But he was the one who'd collapsed. "I wasn't running," Dave admitted. "I was part of the club contingent working on the drinks station."

Hit or Miss

Miss.

Between 2011 and 2015 Marathon Madness was rejected by *The Weekly News*, *My Weekly* and *Best*. It also failed to make the grade in a *Writers' News* competition for stories with a 'racing' theme.

ALL THE LIFT I NEEDED

I pressed the lift button labelled 'GF' and dropped my fixed smile. That awful fiftieth birthday presentation had totally exhausted my cheeriness.

"This will get you a man, Julie," Susie had said, handing me the gift-wrapped parcel in front of all our colleagues. "Even Adam might succumb!"

Everyone had roared with laughter at this remark, including Adam. I wanted to die with embarrassment. Were my feelings for him so obvious and so amusing? Being only three months into this new job I couldn't tell whether people were laughing with me or at me. It didn't help that I hadn't yet started dating again since my divorce - but I had got around to fancying people.

Things got even worse when I tore open the present and showed my naivety about the contents. Susie had then gleefully demonstrated how they should be used.

"I'm not taking my top off to show you properly,"

she'd announced to the group assembled around our desks. "But I never go out without some extra padding and support up top."

Another roar of laughter had filled the room.

Now a black leather shoe appeared between the closing lift doors, forcing them to slide open again. The foot turned into Adam. I couldn't look at him after that terrible birthday scene. Thankfully, he was busy on his phone. Adam and I were the same age. He was like a mature film star, with his craggy, lived-in face, muscular build and a healthy tan. And he was divorced like me.

A sudden thud threw us both off balance. I clutched at the metal rail running around the wall.

"We've stopped." Adam stated the obvious.

"It'll only be for a second." I crossed my fingers.

The seconds turned into a minute. The minute turned into five.

"Where's the emergency button?" Adam moved over to the control panel next to me.

His closeness made me tingle. It was a feeling I wasn't used to and I had to step away. Adam prodded a red button illustrated with a telephone. Nothing happened.

"We'll just have to sit it out." He lowered himself to the floor and closed his eyes.

I was relieved he wanted to doze. What's the protocol for a middle-aged woman who's been out of the dating scene for years but now finds herself trapped in a lift with a man she fancies and in front of whom, she's just been totally embarrassed?

He opened his eyes and smiled. "It's getting warm."

He was right. I was hot and thirsty.

"You don't look too good." Adam sounded concerned. "I saw you put a bottle of water in your bag earlier. I'll get it for you."

The bag was between us on the floor, nearer to Adam.

"No! Let me!" I snatched the bag, scared that wretched present would fall out. I'd stuffed it away as soon as possible but it hardly fitted in the bag with everything else I carried around. As I reached inside, the torn gift-wrapping spewed out and discarded its contents.

Adam started to retrieve the bits and pieces. His fingers caressed the 'oval bust boosters', which resembled chicken rather than human breasts. He stared at the roll of tape and lingered over the fully illustrated instruction leaflet entitled 'Boob Enhancement Kit'.

I tried to make myself invisible.

"Do women really tape themselves up with all this extra padding?" he asked.

I shrugged. This was the end of any chance I had with Adam.

"You don't need enhancing – you look great as you are."

"Thanks," I managed. He got full marks for staying polite, whatever he actually thought about me.

"On my fiftieth last year, they bought me a potion to 'enlarge my manhood'." He used his hands as inverted commas around the phrase. "All I could do was laugh; Susie means none of it personally and she forgets that some of us are more sensitive than others."

I smiled as I imagined how well Adam would've reacted to his birthday presentation. I took a swig of water. Perhaps I'd blown this afternoon and that terrible present out of proportion. Susie had looked hilarious as she held the bra inserts over her blouse and paraded around the office. Perhaps it hadn't been personal at all. Maybe the divorce had sapped more of my confidence than I'd thought.

"Me and you should think up something really gruesome for Susie's thirtieth next month. Do you fancy…" Adam stopped mid-sentence as we felt another thud.

The lift was moving again. In a moment the doors would open and whatever Adam was about to say would be lost forever. Wasn't fifty the new forty? Didn't that mean I got another chance at life beginning? I needed to act before I permanently styled myself as 'divorce victim'.

"Do I fancy what?" I asked and banged my hand against the button labelled 'Emergency Stop' - we needed to finish our conversation.

Adam grinned and winked at me as the lift thudded to a halt again.

Hit or Miss?

Hit!

This story was published in 2014 on the now defunct 'Writing Through divorce' website and earned me $25. The story was inspired by my male co-workers' reaction to finding a Boob Enhancement Kit in a shopping catalogue they were leafing through. They found it hilarious and I realised that giving the kit publicly as a gift could make a highly embarrassing situation.

EMERALD WRITING WORKSHOPS FLASH FICTION

During 2011 and 2012 I entered several flash fiction competitions organised by Eddie Walsh of Emerald Writing Workshops. These competitions had a low entry fee and small prizes and were friendly and fun. I was sorry when they finished. Some of my entries are below. These were all placed or shortlisted in different competitions – can you work out which got the higher rankings?

Like Father, Like Son

1960
"Two boys with the same birth weight – no one need ever know," said Maureen, as she wrote 'Sedgely' on the first blue plastic bracelet. "With luck we might even have got the right band on the right baby."

"I still think we should own up," Sheila muttered as she wrote 'Fitzwilliam' on the second band.

"No - we'll be kicked off the midwifery course – you know what a stickler for protocol Matron is."

1971

"It's hard to believe he's our son." Bert Sedgely looked again at the letter in his hand. "I've never read a book in my life but our Kevin's gone and won himself a scholarship to that posh private school."

"My extra cleaning job will pay for his uniform," said Freda, the glow of maternal pride relaxing her pinched features and making her look almost beautiful.

April 1976

"You must pull your socks up, Quentin!" Julian Fitzwilliam's voice was harsh. "I don't pay a fortune in school fees for you to misbehave in class."

"And the neighbours are complaining," Daphne, Quentin's mother, added. "They don't like the racket you make kicking those tin cans down the road – it's so working class."

"Try making friends with some of the boys at school – their breeding might rub off on you," Julian continued. "Invite one of them home for tea."

May 1976

"This is Kevin." Quentin gestured sullenly at the boy standing behind him in the kitchen doorway.

Daphne looked at the boy and was unable to speak. She gripped the kitchen table and stared at Kevin, a sixteen-year-old version of her husband. She'd known he'd had affairs but had he been careless enough to produce a child?

Later, Julian answered the door when Bert Sedgely came to collect his son. He gawped at the man, unable to speak. Looking at Bert was like looking at a middle-aged version of Quentin. The man had his son's deep-set eyes, slightly weak chin and the same habit of nervously fiddling with his ear lobe.

"Daphne!" Quentin called. "Come and meet Mr Sedgely."

He watched closely as his wife shook hands with the man. Would she be able to hide the fact they'd been lovers sixteen years ago? Was the affair still going on?

Daphne and Julian fought late into the night – each convinced the other had been unfaithful. Next morning, at the end of her tether, Daphne visited the surgery for anti-depressants. She told her tale of woe to the practice nurse.

"What's your son's date of birth?" Sheila asked, twisting her apron in sweaty hands, "and the other boy's surname?"

Daphne told her, adding, "They share the same birthday."

Sheila's heart thundered. "There's something I think you need to know."

A Story of Everyday Train Folk

Every day the same faces boarded the 7:50 to the city. Like clones, they sat in their suits, deliberately avoiding eye contact. Laptops, mobiles, Kindles and headphones cut dead the possibility of any human interaction.

HIT OR MISS?

Until one day a man without a briefcase and not wearing a tie boarded the train. He shuffled along in carpet slippers, carrying a holdall and wearing clothes the colour of grime. The cloned passengers recoiled and concentrated feverishly on their gadgets. No-one risked eye contact with the alien, lest he sat next to them.

A young woman in a pinstripe skirt and jacket wasn't quick enough to use her bag to block the adjacent empty seat. She shuffled closer to the window and held herself stiffly to avoid accidental physical contact with the tramp. He placed the dirty blue holdall on his lap, unzipped the bag an inch and spoke quietly into the opening.

"Not long now, my lovely."

The carriage lowered their electronics and stared at him. Sensing their attention, the man glanced up and around at his fellow passengers. As his eyes grazed each of them, like a Mexican wave they looked down and then up again as his attention moved to the next seat. The trapped pin-stripe lady attempted to ignore her neighbour but started when a high-pitched noise escaped from the bag.

"Don't be scared," the man said and patted her knee. "You're in no danger."

She shot from her seat and, like a circus contortionist, squeezed past the tramp without physical contact with him or the holdall. The word 'danger' flagged red mist in her brain and in the rest of the carriage.

"What's in the bag?" demanded one of the braver suits.

There was a communal intake of breath at the interrogator's heroism and the clones abandoned interest in their personal technology.

"Nothing."

Another high-pitched noise and then the holdall shuddered. The pin-stripe woman's anxiety spread through the close confines of the compartment and passengers muttered to each other in fear.

The ticket collector entered the carriage. The nearest suit grabbed his arm and pointed at the holdall. "Bomb!" he announced in a stage whisper. "It's vibrating – must be ready to explode."

Panic flitted through the air, pin-stripe woman screamed and the ticket collector moved towards the communication cord.

"No!" shouted the tramp and fumbled in his pocket.

"He's pulling a gun," announced the braver suit. "Hit the deck or be shot."

Expensive Saville Row cloth plunged down to the grime carried by a million shoes. Muffled barking accompanied screeching brakes as the train slowed and halted. The tramp looked down in puzzlement at the prone suits.

"It's only a dog biscuit," he said, feeding the canine head that had appeared through the open zip. "She whines and shakes like that when she's hungry."

With sharp movements and angry curses the clones, now slightly red in the face, brushed themselves down and reconnected to their electronic umbilical cords.

<u>Tangled Lives</u>

It's not every day that your boss admits his lust for

you.

It was only the booze talking but a little part of me wants him to be telling the truth. It was like sparks from a Catherine wheel when he touched my knee and, for a second, I felt like a teenager again.

On ordinary days I'm a middle-aged woman who goes about her business invisible to the opposite sex. The children have left and, after thirty years married, John and I fit snugly in the rut we plough through life. He makes the morning tea; I do the bedtime cocoa and on Saturday nights we have a bottle of wine and a Chinese takeaway. Things chug along quite nicely. Or at least they did. I should phone him for a lift before Phillip says or does anything else. It's only a retirement party – no-one will miss me.

Someone bangs on the cubicle door. I've been hiding in the loo too long. I wanted peace and quiet to get a grip on myself.

"Judith?"

That's Emma from accounts.

"Won't be a minute." I flush the loo.

"Phillip sent me to look for you. He says you've been gone ages."

I make heavy work of washing my hands and don't meet Emma's eye.

"You're flushed," she says and then giggles. "Excuse the pun!"

She's under the influence as well.

I don't phone John. I follow Emma back into the Gainsborough suite of the Royal Hotel. Phillip's face lights up as I sit back down beside him. He squeezes my hand under the table cloth.

"Hope I haven't overstepped the mark," he whispers, "with what I said before."

"No. Don't worry about it." What else could I say? I left my hand in his.

Phillip and I have sat alongside each other on our twirly office chairs for nearly 15 years. I've watched the photos on his desk change from school pictures to graduation and then formal wedding portraits. There are no family memorabilia around my PC. As a working mum, I wanted to show my mind was on the job and not worrying about the childminder but it didn't take me long to realise that women can't 'have it all' in the way that men can.

Our hands are still entwined and it feels right.

John will be watching *A Touch of Frost* now. It still it feels right to be holding Phillip's hand. We've probably spent more waking hours together than any married couple. We've got to know each other's quirks, favourite biscuits and views on the world in general. We talk more than John and I.

"I've booked a room."

I feel his breath on my ear.

"But John will …"

"Make an excuse."

I go outside to get a signal. "John. I don't need a lift." Heart thumping, mind racing. "Emma's got a twin room and says I can share."

He mutters something about toothbrushes and nightclothes. I end the call.

<u>An Unfit Bride</u>

Finding a bride for one's only son is difficult. She will eventually become Queen and be responsible for producing and nurturing royal heirs. So, I drew up a list of requirements (in no particular order):

1. Beauty
2. Good Health
3. Maternal
4. Intelligent
5. From a 'well-to-do' background.

Then I organised a ball at the palace and invited all women of noble birth to attend and be presented to the prince. It was a sumptuous evening with dancing, music and fireworks planned until long past midnight. However, as the clock struck twelve things went wrong.

My son, Charming, had spent too long dancing with the same lady and the other guests were becoming restless. I was about to have a word in his ear when this lady sprinted from the ballroom and out into the night. She left behind a glass slipper. Charming was inconsolable.

"She must be my bride," he told me the next morning.

"Very well," I said, anxious to please my love-struck son. "We will scour the land to find the owner of the slipper. If she meets the criteria then you may marry her."

Almost every house in the kingdom had been visited without success when we came across Baron Hardup's run-down manor house. I was reluctant to knock because it was obvious the Baron's daughters would not meet the 'well-to-do' background requirement. They'd only been invited to the ball because the Baron's late first wife had been to school with the Queen.

"Everyone must try on the slipper," Charming insisted. "Besides 'well-to-do' is not an important criterion."

My son had his way.

Hardup's step-daughters were not beautiful, maternal or intelligent. They were clumsy, argumentative and had feet far too big for the dainty glass shoe. The prince looked as relieved as I felt when it did not fit. We were about to depart when a servant girl appeared. Her clothes were ragged and her face grubby with dust.

"Will you try the slipper?" Charming asked her.

"She was not at the ball," I said, anxious to get my son away from this place.

But already the girl was sitting on a stool and removing her wooden clog.

"It fits!" Charming exclaimed with joy and knelt to kiss her hand.

I dragged him to a corner of the room. "She is not well-to-do and will never settle into royal life. Her education will have been minimal – she is unfit to bear your children."

"She is the Baron's natural daughter and therefore of noble birth."

"It is a birth-right lost through her father's financial irresponsibility. I will not allow someone with those genes to marry into the royal family."

"I insist that she becomes my wife."

"Then you are banned from the Palace for evermore and will never become King."

Charming and Cinderella married shortly afterwards and, from the servant grapevine, I hear that they live in a tumbledown cottage and eke out a living by farming the land.

HIT OR MISS?

Emerald Writing Workshops Flash Fiction – Placings

Runner up: An Unfit Bride
Third: Everyday Train Folk
Third: Tangled Lives
Shortlisted: Like Father, Like Son

FRONTLINE RESPONSE

Scott loved his job. He liked arriving at a disaster and using his initiative and skills to avert further crisis. The pay wasn't great but the relief and gratitude expressed by those he helped was a reward in itself. Often, after a call-out, he'd receive a thank you card or a box of chocolates.

Tonight would be the highpoint of Scott's career so far. It was the first time he'd been invited to the Frontline National Awards' Ceremony and his excitement was growing. Only colleagues shortlisted for an award were invited to the slap-up meal in a posh hotel in London. He'd been given overnight accommodation in a hotel room as big as the whole of his flat back home. The famous comedian, Donald Diamond, was hosting the event and the press would be there. The winners would be invited to take part in an early evening chat show the next day to talk about their work. Scott felt nervous at the mere thought of it.

There were two other nominees in his 'Beyond the Call of Duty' category and, like Scott, they'd both gone the extra mile. Just in case he won, Scott had written an acceptance speech and the sheet of paper was now folded safely in the pocket of his dinner jacket. In ten minutes he'd go down to the hotel ballroom where the ceremony was being held. As he fastened the laces of his new black shoes, he remembered the meeting when his boss had told him about the nomination.

"How you saved that lady in Station Road was way beyond the call of duty," his manager had said. "It deserves wider recognition and will be an excellent public relations opportunity for us too."

That Station Road incident would live in Scott's memory for a long time. A little girl had answered the door, tears streaming down her face.

"Where's Mummy?" Scott had asked. The control centre had told him the initial call had been made by a Mrs Castle.

"In the kitchen," the little girl said. "She's on the floor. She's got low blood pressure and it makes her dizzy. Will you make everything better?"

Scott was taken aback by the medical information and he knew better than to promise he could make everything OK. Most incidents had a happy ending but there were odd ones where it was immediately obvious nothing could be done. Breaking bad news was the hardest part of the job, especially to those who had been given false hope.

"I'll do my best. Can you take me to your mum?"

"She's the coach for the school rounders team," the little girl continued her delivery of information as she led Scott through the hallway. "She drives the minibus to matches and washes our kit and everything. We're in the cup final tomorrow. We won't miss it, will we?" Her face crumpled into tears once more.

"I hope not." Scott patted the little girl on the shoulder. "Now, let's see how Mummy is."

Mrs Castle was lying on her stomach in front of the washing machine. Scott knelt down next to her. She groaned and struggled to roll over. The little girl sat down on the vinyl floor and held her mother's hand. The woman gave a sob.

"Sit up slowly," Scott said. "That way you'll go less dizzy."

Mrs Castle pushed herself up, shifted away from the washing machine and sat with her back against the wall. She looked pale. He hoped she wouldn't faint.

"Mummy was getting our rounders tops ready for tomorrow," the little girl explained and then sniffled again.

Scott could see the water level halfway up the inside of the bulbous glass window of the washer. The machine gave a sudden jerk and made a burping noise. The little girl had laughed then, despite her tears.

If Scott won the 'Beyond the Call of Duty' award and got invited on that chat show, the call-out to Mrs Castle was the one he would talk about. The little girl had reminded him of his niece and he'd been touched by the way she put all her trust in him. With Mrs Castle still leaning against the kitchen wall Scott had done his preliminary examination and realised the situation was serious. There was nothing more he could do on the spot.

"I'm only a first-responder," he explained to Mrs Castle, who was now taking small sips of water from a glass delivered by her daughter. "This is beyond what I can deal with."

Mrs Castle groaned. "The rounders match ... I can't let the girls down."

There'd been one more thing which Scott could do that might help. He'd gone out to his car for more equipment. Then he'd helped Mrs Castle to her feet and guided her to a chair at the kitchen table. As he'd uncoiled a length of plastic tube he'd winked at the little girl.

Scott's borrowed bow tie was on elastic and felt uncomfortably tight around his neck in the warmth of the ballroom, but he needed to look the part for his moment of glory. He'd hired the dinner suit especially for the occasion and it made him walk tall and feel proud.

"Now we come to our final award of the evening," Donald Diamond announced. "The Beyond the Call of Duty Award."

He read out the three nominees and explained what each had done to merit a shortlisting for the £1000 prize. Scott's hands were clammy with nerves and he had his fingers crossed on both hands.

"And the winner is," started Donald. There was complete silence as he left a tension building pause. "Scott Brown for the Station Road incident!"

The room filled with applause. Hardly believing he was the winner, Scott squeezed between chairs and tables on his way up to the platform. People were patting him on the back, his heart was thumping and he was panicking at the thought of addressing this room full of people. On the stage Donald Diamond shook Scott's hand and presented him with an engraved glass trophy and a cheque. Then there was silence as the audience waited for Scott to speak. The carefully crafted acceptance speech had flown from his mind. His hands were full with the trophy and the large envelope containing the cheque. Retrieving the speech notes from his pocket was impossible. Scott managed only a few words, thanking his colleagues and his superiors for their help.

But on the chat show the following evening he was calmer, prepared and able to explain in detail the action he'd taken at Station Road. He told the presenter how he'd drained the faulty washing machine and called a doctor to check Mrs Castle. She'd been lying on the floor trying to identify the machine's drain hole herself before Scott arrived. Then he'd taken the dripping rounders kit to his own home, washed and dried it and delivered it to the school the next day before the cup final match.

The chat show host looked impressed. "Thank you, Scott," she said, "for being another example of how Frontline's washing machine repairmen are our modern knights in shining armour!

Hit or Miss?

Hit!

Frontline Response was published in *The Weekly News* in 2017.

RENOUNCING THE EMPIRE

London - 2:00 am 8th December 1936

Darling Wallis, is she awake or asleep? Is she restless like me, unable to still a racing mind? Do the same bright stars that sneak through the curtains of my bedroom also scatter silver on her eiderdown? I wish so much that I hadn't sent her away at the very time I most need her. It was to save her sanity. Since the news of our relationship reached the press, she's been hounded by all and sundry. Dear Wallis, she deserves much better than this and is finding the entire furore hard to bear. At least in France, for the time being, she is sheltered from all the madness here. I spoke to her on the telephone this evening.

"David," she said, "please consider things thoroughly one last time. I will think no less of you if you decide that your future lies with the crown. In fact, it will be of some relief to me - I am worried that

I cannot possibly take the place of a whole empire in your life."

"Sweetheart!" I had to raise my voice above the crackles on the line but I hope she still sensed the affection in my voice and not my annoyance with the interference on our call. "My Empress is all I need to be happy - and that is you. Whether or not we have an empire doesn't matter a jot - but I would like a little land so that we can sit outside with our cocktails and watch the sun go down together."

"But I don't have my decree nisi yet." I caught the anxiety in her seductive American lilt. "You know the English divorce laws - it may never be granted and then you will have neither your role as king nor me as your wife."

I tried to reassure her that whatever happened, we would always be together. I think she took some comfort from that but now, how I long to hold her close, smell her spicy perfume and comfort her properly.

Tomorrow I will give Mr Baldwin my decision and put an end to all this hurtful speculation and gossip. When I listen to my heart, life with Wallis is the only way forward. When I listen to my head, I know that I cannot properly carry out the duties of a king without the support of the woman I love. But still my decision is not made. Mr Baldwin outlined three possible choices for me and now, in these dark hours before dawn, with sleep a million miles away, I wrestle with them for the last time - trying to find a way through.

I cannot even consider the prime minister's first option - finish my relationship with Mrs Simpson. That is out of the question.

His second option is attractive to the reckless

gambler in my soul. The stakes are high and, if it didn't pay off, I would be inflicting losses on a whole nation of people. "If you marry that woman against the wishes of the government, then all your ministers will resign immediately," Baldwin warned me in a tone that indicated he wasn't bluffing. "It is one of your options but I wouldn't advise it."

How can he be so sure what all the other cabinet members will do once their backs are against the wall? Baldwin and a few others might feel principled enough to abandon their careers but there'd surely be others who would be only too keen to step into their empty shoes and have a chance to run the country. It's such a great temptation to marry Wallis and be damned! With her at my side I could continue confidently as monarch. But can I risk leaving the country without a government?

I throw back the eiderdown and get out of bed. It's cold but the chill will sharpen my brain. I stand at the window and look out over the shadowy grounds. Over the years, this view has grown familiar to me, at all times of day and through all seasons.

There's the tree that Bertie and I climbed as boys. Once we constructed a rope swing over one of the branches - when Father wasn't at home to scold us. Father went out of his way to make us fear him. Bertie suffered the most with his stammer, his knock knees and his left-handedness. He'll suffer again if I take the third option that Baldwin gave me - abdication. Then Bertie would take my place on the throne. He would do it without question but how hard he would find it. He isn't a confident extrovert like me but he does have what I would lack, the support of a close and loving wife. Elizabeth has already berated me several times for my dereliction of duty and she barely tolerates Wallis. She is like a lioness with cubs as she tries to protect her beloved Bertie.

The stars are bright tonight - as though they want me to see everything and remember this view in years to come, when I no longer have the right to live here.

Whatever decision I give to Baldwin tomorrow, there will be suffering. I should try to sleep now, in these hours that remain before dawn.

France - 2:00 am 8th December 1936
David sounded irritated on the telephone this evening, whether that was with me personally or with this whole damn business, I couldn't tell. The line was appalling but I gathered he will give Baldwin his decision tomorrow. Unless David has suddenly come to his senses, he will abandon his royal duty.

What a dreadful obligation such a decision will place on me. The anxiety is driving me insane. Sleep is impossible. How can marriage to me replace a whole empire for him? What will happen when I lose my looks and the sex isn't great anymore?

Before the old King died, being courted, wined, dined and partied by the Prince of Wales was such a fantastical adventure. It was a leg up into proper society. But I never expected it to last nor to lead to such a massive commitment. For me, after only a few years, life with the same man becomes tiresome. If I could walk away now I would, but David threatened suicide if I should ever leave him. There is no escape route.

Meanwhile, England, and probably the whole Empire, detests me. They forget that bedding the

King of England wasn't my doing alone. David always knew I was a married woman with a previous divorce. My two failed marriages paint me as the villain of the piece, whilst David's earlier liaisons are over-looked because they never had an official stamp.

As I wrote in my last letter to Ernest, "I feel so small and licked by it all."

Sometimes I wonder why he and I are divorcing at all. We get along alright most of the time, it was just that, for me, as usual, the grass looked greener elsewhere. A taste of society and some adventure before middle-age claimed me - was that too much to ask? I never meant to steal the King of England. David's feelings quickly became deeper than I anticipated, things got out of control and, instead of being his playmate, now the chains of lifelong obligation are snapping around my wrists and ankles. Is it any wonder that the peace of sleep will not descend? I lie here and stare at the scatter of silver on my eiderdown. The stars are bright tonight.

If David renounces the throne tomorrow, as I'm sure he will, Elizabeth will get her poisonous claws even deeper into me. Her precious Bertie will be forced to conquer his shyness and learn to speak publicly. It will do him good to stop hiding behind his brother and wife.

But such a decision will do me no good whatsoever - I will be ostracised from society and forced to live a quiet life somewhere, with the only king in English history who abdicated voluntarily. It is a compliment that he wants to marry me more than he wants an empire. But I don't want to marry into royalty if I can't enjoy all the trappings and trimmings that come with it. A life in exile is no good to me.

RENOUNCING THE EMPIRE

I abandon my quest for sleep and go to the window. It's cold and I pull a dressing gown around me. I'd like to think that David is staring at this same starry sky and pale moon. But he'll be sleeping. A long time ago he vowed never to give me up. We've all tried to change his mind over the past weeks - me, Baldwin and Elizabeth - but he doesn't listen. He tried to have the best of both worlds by asking Baldwin for permission to broadcast an appeal to the nation. He wanted to persuade the people to allow him to remain king after marrying me. He didn't get his broadcast.

David will let the Empire go, not me. He will be sleeping easy tonight, with his decision made. I can't sleep because he's decided my future too - without ever properly listening to what I want.

How can one woman be a whole empire to a man?

Hit or Miss?

Miss.

This story failed to make the grade in five competitions between 2013 and 2016. It was inspired by a Writer's News competition with the theme, 'Insomnia'.

OLD COMEDIANS NEVER DIE

Standing in the wings, Ian felt the familiar buzz of excitement, anticipation and terror. This was the moment he loved, the adrenaline coursing through his body before he stepped into the limelight. It surpassed every other high point in his life, including the birth of his sons and his wedding day. For these few seconds he felt like a young man again, capable of anything. He had the bliss of forgetting his body was ageing quicker than his mind.

His wife, Sandra, didn't understand. She hadn't wanted him to perform tonight.

"It's your seventieth birthday," she'd said. "Let somebody else take the strain. Spend some time with us for a change whilst you're still able. Sometimes I think you forget you've got a family."

At the very least Sandra wanted him to announce his retirement tonight. She wanted them to be together, go on days out with the grandchildren, take an extended winter holiday in the sun and get involved with village activities. Sandra would never understand how it felt to be surrounded by laughter and applause after a one-liner hit just the right spot. It was a drug which kept dragging the addict back for more. Nothing could match that pleasure of manipulating audiences. With a little bit of practice, a good comedian could always find a crowd's funny bone and slowly tickle it to death. And the fear of failure made the high of success even sweeter.

Ian had started on the pub and club circuit as an occasional schoolboy stooge for his uncle. Being the public butt of the older man's jokes had been his training ground. He watched his uncle deal with hecklers and those the worse for drink. Then, just after Ian got his first proper job on a car assembly line, his uncle had a massive heart attack. The *Duck Arms,* where they were due to play that evening, had insisted the show must go on to avoid a riot among the punters who were expecting a Friday night turn. Ian had to perform alone for the very first time.

He'd thrown up twice in the pub toilet beforehand and begged the landlord to find a replacement for him. As he washed his face for a second time, he heard the growing "Why are we waiting?" chant from the audience. The landlord dragged him onto the stage and introduced him.

Silence followed. For a few seconds Ian prayed for a heart attack to take him too. Then his uncle's well-worn routine popped into his head and he was away, mimicking the dead man's act as closely as possible without a stooge of his own.

With the benefit of years of hindsight, he knew much of his timing had been wrong and that he'd gabbled too quickly. However, the audience had been well-oiled and in a good mood – it was the start of the local factory's summer shutdown. The applause at the end had gone straight to Ian's head. For the first time that appreciation was for him alone – it was the beginning of his addiction. The next day he'd immediately offered to take over all his uncle's future bookings. The factory job had been consigned to history.

Ian peeked out at tonight's audience. They were in a church hall with a stage more used to pantomimes and gospel choirs than comedians. Everyone was dressed up and looking expectant. He recognised the gaggle of youngsters sitting down the front. They were giggling already and fighting over a bag of sweets. An unhappy-looking Sandra was sitting next to her sister and brother-in-law. Ian had overheard one side of a telephone conversation between the two women the previous week.

"He's pushing himself too hard," Sandra had said. "All those late nights and driving home in the early hours. He has to spend most of the next day sleeping. You'd think that at his age he'd be happy to let someone else take over. The world is full of wannabe performers. I wish he'd stayed on that car production line."

There'd been a short pause whilst Sandra had let her sister slip a word in edgeways then she'd continued. "Yes, I know this gig is a bit different. But that's precisely *why* I don't want him to do it. It's his birthday, I want him to relax and spend the evening with me for a change. Most men are happy to collect their carriage clock and call it a day when they hit sixty-five but Ian won't give up the stage until he's in a wooden box. And the way he's going that might be sooner rather than later – remember what happened to his uncle, and he was much younger."

Looking at Sandra in the audience now, a wave of guilt diluted Ian's anticipation of the performance. She was the only singleton in a row of couples. During their decades of marriage they'd spent more nights apart than together. He'd toured the country doing gigs and she'd brought up the children. He'd never made the big time despite a brief appearance in the '80s revival of *New Faces*. But he'd always earned enough to feed, clothe and house his family – even if he was rarely there to share it with them.

"It's not too late to back out," Sandra had said to him this morning. "You've got plenty of contacts who'd do tonight for you. And they'd take your future bookings – you'd be leaving nobody in the lurch."

They'd be like beady-eyed vultures, thought Ian. They'd be fighting over his diary to snatch all those regular gigs he'd built up over the years. He couldn't bear all that hard work being presented to someone else on a plate, least of all to people who he felt were inferior to himself.

Sandra had squeezed both his hands and stared up at him with pleading eyes. It was a long time since he'd looked at her properly. When someone is so familiar, you hardly register them changing and ageing. Now he realised that the beautiful young woman he'd married had been replaced by his mother-in-law (a good line for his act – he made a mental note). The same grey hair, powdered skin and generous waistline which had characterised the older woman the first time Sandra had taken him home for tea. Perhaps, likewise, he'd become the image of his father. He felt a pang for all the years that had gone by without him noticing her. She'd matured quietly and gracefully.

It was only recently that she'd started to kick up a fuss about his workload. He'd had chest pains after coming off stage in Scarborough last year. There'd been no need to fuss but someone had called an ambulance. The doctors had inserted a couple of stents and he'd felt as right as rain. But Sandra had been left constantly anxious. Even so he hadn't given into her pleas to back out of tonight's gig but perhaps he would fulfil her expectations by making an announcement about his future tonight.

"Alright, Dad?" Ian's eldest son strode past him onto the stage to introduce his father's act. "Ready for your public?"

Ian nodded.

"Ladies and Gentlemen, we have a very special turn for you tonight – performing at his own seventieth birthday party - the birthday boy himself, Ian Holdsworth!"

Ian made his entrance and had to wait two full minutes for the standing ovation to subside. The hall was decorated with banners and balloons emblazoned with '70' and, from the stage, he could see straight into the kitchen at the back of the large room where white-coated caterers were setting up the buffet that Sandra had agonised over for weeks.

Then, for a second, that same silence from his first solo gig hung in the church hall. He was aware of his heartbeat. So far so good with the stents. Words scrambled around Ian's head as he tried to phrase the formal announcement that Sandra wanted to hear. Retirement. Last gig. Spend more time with the family. But none of them made it to his mouth. Doing this was what made him feel more alive than anything. For Ian, giving up the stage would be like lying down with a plastic bag over his head.

He blew a kiss to Sandra and launched into his first joke.

Hit or Miss?

Miss.

'Old Comedians Never Die' failed to make the grade in five competitions between 2012 and 2017. It was inspired by the theme for the Swanwick Writers' Summer School Competition 2012, which had the theme '65 Not Out' to celebrate sixty-five years of the school. The original version of the story was based around Ian's 65th birthday. In this version I changed it to 70 to reflect the rising state pension age and the fact that many people in show business carry on performing to a ripe old age.

NOBODY'S HERO

Ian handed me a steaming mug and a mince pie. "A strong coffee, Debbie, plus something sweet to perk you up."

Five a.m. on Christmas Day and we were into the last couple of hours of the nightshift. The TV in the corner of the office was showing the early morning festive news. There was a clip of our MP doing his annual visits to the emergency services. He was shaking hands with firemen, giving the police a pat on the back and joking with an ambulance crew. Finally, there were bouquets for nurses on an intensive care ward.

My mobile rang. It was Amy.

"Santa's been, Mummy! We tried to wait for you to come home but it was too difficult. He brought me a doll with three different outfits and a feeding bottle."

Tears pricked at the corners of my eyes. My six-year-old chattered on about colouring books, chocolate reindeer and the other stocking fillers she'd unwrapped in my absence. I silently mourned what I'd missed whilst on duty. I didn't even have the satisfaction of being a life-saver. I was just an absent mummy and nobody's hero.

"Love you too, darling," I whispered as Amy ended the call.

"Never comes here, does he?" Ian pointed at the TV. "More people rely on us over the holiday season than will end up in A and E or have their houses burned down."

"Thankfully," I murmur. I didn't begrudge the emergency services their honourable visitor but I did mind the lack of appreciation for my Christmas sacrifice.

"Imagine the uproar if our main computer server went down," Ian continued, "and we weren't here to pick up the pieces."

I nodded. I can't believe how addicted to internet shopping people have become. No sooner are all the presents bought and wrapped than the online sales start and people are busy clicking and filling virtual baskets in between checking the turkey and making the gravy. But all these websites don't look after themselves. We have staff here 24/7 to sort out glitches and keep everything running smoothly - even when the rest of the country is stuffing themselves with sherry and Quality Street.

Suddenly a crimson warning message flashed up on the screen in front of us.

"All systems go!" Ian declared. "People are getting up and the website traffic's increasing. Check capacity, please."

"No."

Ian gave me an odd look. I stared back at him and slowly ate my mince pie.

"Debbie, we have to do something otherwise the website will crash."

"Let it." I drain my coffee. Lack of sleep combined with caffeine and sugar was making me defiant.

"What's got into you? The online sale started fifteen minutes ago. Thousands of people want to shop."

"It's Christmas morning, Ian! Nobody will die if they can't order a new sofa or choose a dining table."

The computer console bleeped and another red message flashed up. Ian's hand reached towards the keyboard and I pulled it back.

"I want people to know we exist," I said.

One minute later a series of flashing messages rolled up the screen. The *Furniture Chest* website had crashed.

"Leave it ten minutes," I instructed. "Then we'll check the company's Twitter feed."

"Senior management will find out."

"That's my plan."

Very soon there were several tweets from irate customers. Then the office phone rang. I grabbed the receiver before Ian. The sales director was seriously panicky.

"Yes, we are aware and we're working on bringing the website back." I reassured him calmly. "No, the crash couldn't have been foreseen. It was all to do with the massive popularity of the sale."

Replacing the receiver, I nodded to Ian that he could now put things right. "But take your time. Make those directors sweat a little first."

Then the sales director tweeted: 'Furniture Chest website crash: Our wonderful tech guys & girls are on the case. Problem will be fixed soon by our own Christmas HEROES!'

Ian punched the air. I grinned and pressed 'Retweet'. Officially becoming a hero didn't compensate for missing Amy's Christmas morning but it made me feel better. And Ian was looking at me with respect - something that I hoped would last into the New Year.

Hit or Miss?

Hit!

A version of this story was published in *My Weekly* in December 2015 under the title, 'All Systems Down'. The inspiration came from my own experience on Boxing Day 2014. I work in IT and was called out in the early hours to help fix a problem. Modern life means increasing numbers of us are required to work through the festive period and many of these Christmas workers are invisible. Until something goes wrong, we don't know they exist but they deserve some recognition.

ADAPTING NOT CHEATING

Tracey had the folded piece of paper in her pocket. Six numbers, each one within a perfect circle. She'd written out the same numbers every week for twenty-six years. At first she'd used her daughter's wax crayons to colour each circle to match the balls in Arthur, Guinevere, Lancelot and Merlin. Then she switched to felt tips, bought especially for the job: blue, pink, green and yellow, plus her own birthday circle which had to be left white. Now she used her grandson's coloured pencils for the shading. Recently purple numbers had been introduced too but Tracey hadn't changed her selection to include any between 50 and 59, nor had she incorporated the new generation's birth dates. Altering things would spoil the magic of the ritual that had kept her sane for over a quarter of a century. Some might call it cheating but Tracey called it adapting.

She was nearly at the community hall now. Geoff

would be putting chairs in a circle. Jean would be laying out mugs and chocolate biscuits. How would they react when they heard about the money? Would they condemn her for cheating or admire her adaptation of a bad habit into a coping mechanism?

"Tracey! Decant the milk into a jug, please?" Jean looked up from fiddling with a packet of doilies.

It seemed irrelevant to the group's purpose whether the milk was in a floral china jug or its original plastic container. However, presentation was important to Jean and the members were sensitive to what was needed to help each other. That was why Tracey wanted to share her winnings with the group.

As always, she'd watched the draw live on YouTube. Without the live draw, where was the excitement, the adrenaline and the hope? Tracey wanted thrills in exchange for her two pound coin. Correction: she needed thrills or she'd relapse into that awful black loop of debt.

"What's with the big smile, Trace?" Geoff asked.

"I've got important news."

"You want to go first today?"

She nodded. When everyone was assembled Geoff gave her the go ahead.

"I've won the lottery!" It was the first time she'd said it aloud and she couldn't stop grinning.

There was a terrible silence until Geoff spoke coldly. "Members of Gamblers' Recovery Support don't play the lottery."

"Not the actual lottery." Tracey tripped over her words trying to explain that she put £2 in a jar instead of buying a ticket and now her numbers were up she could spend the £2,500 she'd saved. "There's enough for us all to go to London for the weekend."

Silence. Everyone was looking to Geoff for guidance.

"I was adapting. Not cheating." Please make them believe her, she wanted the group to share her prize.

Jean stood up. "The definition of gambling is taking risky action in the hope of a desired result. Tracey's money didn't leave the house. It wasn't a risk."

Cheers ricocheted round the room. Tracey's adaptation had been a good bet.

Hit or Miss?

Miss.

'Adapting not Cheating' failed to make the grade in three competitions between 2019 and 2022. Possibly because gambling addiction is a serious issue and should be addressed as such. Tracey's method of coping may fall outside the boundaries of what is acceptable.

LAST WORD

Thank you for reading *Hit or Miss?* I do hope you've enjoyed it.

I'd love to know whether you agree with the 'Hit' or 'Miss' verdicts in this book and if there is a particular story that you enjoyed, or perhaps a character that stood out for you. If you are happy to share your thoughts on the Amazon review page of *Hit or Miss?* (without spoilers!) that would be fantastic.

You might also enjoy my bumper 'box set' short story book: *A Coffee Break Story Collection*. It contains thirty-six short stories which appeared in magazines or were successful in competitions. Enjoy tales with a twist, contest-winning prose plus gentler slices of life, with a hint of romance. It's available in paperback and for Kindle from Amazon.

Join Sally's newsletter: http://eepurl.com/AHkMP

Follow Sally Jenkins on Twitter: @sallyjenkinsuk

Find her on Facebook: https://www.facebook.com/SallyJenkinsAuthor

Find out more about Sally and follow her blog at http://www.sally-jenkins.com.

Novels by Sally Jenkins

The Promise

A man has been stabbed. A woman is bloodstained. The nightmares from her teenage years have begun again for Olivia Field – just as she is preparing to marry.

Ex-convict, Tina is terminally ill. Before she dies, the care of her younger, psychologically unwell brother, Wayne must be ensured. So Tina calls in a promise made to her thirty years ago in a prison cell. A promise that was written down and placed with crucial evidence illustrating a miscarriage of justice in a murder case.

The Promise is a fast-paced psychological thriller told from several viewpoints. It explores the lengths to which people are prepared go in order to protect those they love and the impossibility of ever fully escaping our past actions.

Reviewers' praise for The Promise:
"I didn't see the ending coming." – Hellymart.
"I quickly found myself in the "I'll just read one more chapter" loop." – Whiskas Mum.
"A brilliant, pacey thriller with an interesting plot line." – Bookliterati.

Available on Kindle.

Bedsit Three

A girl has been buried in a shallow grave. Rain washes away the earth covering her. Bedsit Three is a thrilling why-dunnit which twists and turns its way to a shattering finale! No one knows what goes on behind closed doors or in the darkness of our minds. Sometimes the threat is too close to home …

Bedsit Three is a tale of murder, mystery and love. It won the inaugural Wordplay Publishing/Ian Govan Award and was shortlisted for both the Silverwood-Kobo-Berforts Open Day Competition and the Writing Magazine/McCrit Competition.
Michael Barton, Founder and Managing Director of WordPlay Publishing said of Bedsit Three, "It's a book that elicits emotional reaction, drawing the reader into the story and placing him or her in the middle of the action page after page. Be prepared for a sleepless night, because you won't want to put it down until you get to the end."

Reviewers' praise for Bedsit Three:
"A psychological why dunnit reminiscent of Barbara Vine/ Ruth Rendell. Highly recommended!" Elizabeth Barnsley
"A dark, fairly gritty drama with a side plot of insanity and murder - I enjoyed it!" – Terry Tyler

Available in paperback from Amazon and on Kindle.

Printed in Great Britain
by Amazon